A Sharp Tooth in the Fur

A Sharp Tooth in the Fur

DARRYL WHETTER

GOOSE LANE

Edited by Laurel Boone.
Cover photograph: Tanya Canam, copyright 2002. Reproduced with
permission.
Author photo: University of Windsor
Cover and book design by Julie Scriver.
Printed in Canada by Transcontinental.
10 9 8 7 6 5 4 3 2 1

National Library of Canada Cataloguing in Publication

Whetter, Darryl, 1971-
A sharp tooth in the fur / Darryl Whetter.

ISBN 0-86492-353-8

I. Title.

PS8595.H387S43 2003   C813'.6   C2003-900521-6
PR9199.3.W4284S43 2003

Published with the financial support of the Canada Council for the Arts, the
Government of Canada through the Book Publishing Industry Development
Program, and the New Brunswick Culture and Sports Secretariat.

Goose Lane Editions
469 King Street
Fredericton, New Brunswick
CANADA E3B 1E5
www.gooselane.com

For Linda Bartlett,
who saved me two-and-a-half times.

Contents

You want just one thing: to know the world
so you can go back to it.

— *Tim Lilburn*

Profanity Issues, S.

Russel Metz stands in front of a large half-empty book-case. Beside his feet sits a full whisky box of books. Others line the walls. He doesn't look away, let alone move, until the phone's third ring.

"Mr. Metz, it's Principal Wellsley. I'm afraid we've got a problem with Spenser."

"Is Spenser hurt?"

"No, no, he's fine. It's profanity, Mr. Metz."

Russell smiles and returns to his shelving.

"Spenser has profanity issues."

"Profanity, yes. What's the trouble?"

"I've taken time out, Mr. Metz, to phone you about your son. He's been swearing again."

"The f-word? That sort of problem?"

"Exactly."

"Say it or write it?"

"He was overheard using the word freely in the playground."

"I've endeavoured to promote oral culture."

"Mr. Metz, I'm aware of Spenser's current challenges at home —"

"Technically that's Dr. Metz."

"I'm aware of Spenser's home situation. When can you get away from work?"

"Name a time."

The phone is tossed into a deep, yellow couch Russell hasn't finished paying for, and the latest stack of books is abandoned to the nearest shelf. Spense should be returning shortly. Russell steps away to brush his teeth. Dinner. Dishes. Maybe the grant application if he's not too tired.

"Hey Dad. Home."

Russell doesn't mention the shouting. Spenser still announces himself as if he were entering the William Street house, calling to Dad submerged in the claw-foot tub or Mom in the upstairs office.

"So, the mail?" Spenser asks.

"No contracts from Harvard. No big bills."

"You really apply to Harvard?"

"No, no positions. Not a one. And you, my guy, want to talk about school?"

"Understaffed. Lacks resources and clear direction. Short-sighted."

"Okay, little parrot. How about you and school, today?"

"Fuck," Spenser confesses, whispering melodramatically from the back of his throat and spreading his hands like an impeached but resolute politician.

"You see the inconveniences here?"

"I yam what I yam." Spenser apes a Popeye he's never seen.

"Marks aren't slipping?"

Imitating the overweight comic-book clerk from *The Simpsons*, Spenser hits every syllable with an apathetic deadpan, "Ahh, my bookish friend, gravity weakens in the stratosphere."

"Fix your brain a drink? Milk straight up? Figgers on the side?"

"Coke?"

"C'mon, I got a reputation."

"Milk me. Can I go on-line?"

"Sure, I've had my phone excitement for the day. Print my Outreach stuff while you're on."

Russell reaches into the fridge as the stuck-pig squeals of a modem blurt out from the long room that is both Spenser's bedroom and Russell's office. When he delivers plate and glass he sees that Spenser has drawn back the giant separating curtain. A faux-silk Chinese dragon print in mauve on his side, heavy forest green on Spenser's. Expensive, well-hung, but still curtain playing wall.

Returning to stove and sink, Russell stems spinach and pierces sausages. Hydrates a pilaf. Sets out glasses and the Value Village plates. Russell and Kim had various problems. Young marriage, early child. Russell finishing his Ph.D., Kim articling, then suddenly keen to make junior partner. Infant Spenser was bounced on knees over briefs and essays, passed off between court and night class. Idealists in wool and denim became young professionals with palpitating hearts and sleep deprivation. Sure, they no longer tore open packages of rubber gloves and brought each other off standing in front of the kitchen sink, fingers and skin squeaking delight, but they were a team. They grew. They changed. They were Spenser's.

"Let's be clear here, Dr. Metz, Spenser's profanity is an issue of policy, not ideology."

"That's sealed, then?"

"Spenser breaks the rules. Younger children are corrupted."

"Who, whoa, whoa. My son isn't pushing dope, he's speaking."

"Cursing."

"Touching people through laughter."

"Encouraging rudeness, insolence —"

"Self-reflection. Power sensitivity —"

"Disobedience, flagrant disobedience. Dr. Metz, order is required."

"At what cost? He's a bright, funny kid."

Wellsley leans forward. "Humour can be a mask, though, can't it?"

"Do the words free speech ever come up at your PD days, Mr. Wellsley?"

Wellsley's lips tighten. He breathes. "Let's refocus."

Friends and even soccer parents have told Russell about Wellsley's Christian days. He juts his chin forward. "Tell me how it's wrong."

Exhaling, Wellsley reaches for a red file folder at his elbow, opens it. A computer-printed label on the tab reads *Profanity*, and each face is covered with wide overlapping Post-its, thin yellow shingles layered with cramped blue handwriting. Wellsley slides his fingers through the dense collection, peels one up and passes it over his desk.

> Lick ass, shit teeth.
> — Tom Protter, age 8
> *Miss Langman's class*

Immediately Russell admires the fulfillment of *teeth*. Take on this thing, become this thing. Nice hit, Tommy. Calming, he finally notices the little ship's steering wheel clock and pen set on the desk. The family portrait is flesh and acrylics from frame to frame. Sons thick in the jaw. A grinning wife with large bead earrings and an oatmeal bear-and-snowflake sweater.

"This" — Russell waves the note — "this is a problem of disrespect, not diction."

Wellsley has another specimen ready and quickly rips it free. His eyes actually gleam.

"You're not going to shock me." Russell exchanges notes.

> **Suck a nut, dickless.**
> **— Mike Strachen, age 11**
> **Mr. Brander's class**

"Little Mike has a gift. No, stop." Russell holds a palm up at Wellsley's next specimen. "We're not here to discuss Mike Strachen or young Tommy. These are examples of children being confrontational or verbally abusive. That's not Spenser."

"Foul language is foul language."

"Whoa, did I just step into a Circular Logic Fair?"

"I had hoped you were here to help Spenser."

"Help him to what?"

"Clean up his language."

"Principal Wellsley, life is sometimes filthy, so is language. Spenser articulating himself is about the best help Spenser can get."

"For his parents' divorce, you mean?"

Russell's tongue darts to his lips. "Free your mind, *Mr.* Wellsley, and the rest will follow." Russell hasn't stormed out of a principal's office in almost twenty years.

Jerking open the kitchen door of his apartment, Russell lays his toffee-coloured briefcase aside and heads for the other door, the door with the mail slot. Russell lives in the penumbra between the crushing work of his recently completed Ph.D. and the uncertainty of job interviews. He's hunted possible positions, queried department heads and smothered the world with his curriculum vitae and what must surely be glowing letters of reference. Scraping together a living by coaching writing skills, Russell hangs on the mail every day, endures the weekends, dreads a holiday Monday. Working from home, he knows his envelopes by ear. The deep plangent splash of a nine-by-twelve. The quick plink of the business envelope.

Standing over the pile of today's mail, he's a ten-year-old selecting the first bite of Halloween candy. He sorts, rises and turns back into the room in one fluid motion. University of British Columbia, small envelope.

He speed-dials a number.

"Kim, two minutes."

"Yeah, shoot."

"Could we switch weeks, end of next month? You know there's only one reason I'd ask. Interview with UBC."

"Hey, congratulations. Vancouver, eh?"

"Last time I checked."

"Lotus land." *Vancouver,* her silence says, *thirty-five hundred kilometres away. Huge rents. Less cash to fly.*

Ten years into a ten-year plan, Russell is a mess. His research was strong, his teaching superb. He should feel poised. The tenure-track job for which he has prepared himself tirelessly will now cut him to pieces. For a time it was easier not knowing

where they would settle. Kingston for the Ph.D. and then. . . .
The perfect excuse for never planting a garden, building a com-
post heap or bringing a dog home from the pound. Nicer laundry
hampers or a new dish rack didn't make sense and could still be
called bourgeois. It would be a sacrifice for Kim to switch cities,
firms. Russell felt guilty and touched.

But Kim anchored. Discussions about her not wanting to
leave and his having to move trailed off or were stopped short.
Russell's income was repeatedly clarified. His lack of benefits was
noted. Why have another child when they couldn't afford private
school for Spenser? The early thirties suddenly felt like the
fulcrum of life, and talk only accomplished so much. Once post-
structurally savvy, each of them had now fully discovered the
indisputability of their feelings for Spense. Here it was, love so
simple. She could piss him off. He could disappoint her, as did
the boy. But each of them would always forgive Spenser. They
agreed to joint custody without the drain of a trial.

Russell tries correcting assignments. Nothing helps. Not a
pint of stout. Not Nina Simone's buttery vocals. Sentence frag-
ments jam under his nails like splinters. Overburdened commas
uncouple and spill their sorry loads. Semicolons flicker like ran-
dom Christmas tinsel. The pattern of Wellsley's necktie repeats
itself behind his eyes. When he remembers the office, Russell
now sees a crucifix on the wall.

Tapping his computer awake, he reaches for the local fax
directory.

Free the Tongue to Free the Mind

All choice of words is slang. It marks a class. And the strongest slang of all is the slang of poets. — George Eliot

As soon as you deal with sex explicitly, you are forced to choose between the language of the nursery, the gutter and the anatomy class. — C.S. Lewis

My son's school principal is punishing him for swearing. Darling C.S. Lewis (who gave us the Narnia stories) is right, of course, subjects often demand a specific discourse. Our so-called swear words serve many subjects with an elasticity, brevity or humour otherwise unmatched in our lexicon. To pretend, as the self-righteous do and will, that language should be prohibited is to deny not only self-expression, but also class. Forbid swearing and we forbid life, all for an absurd and affected delicacy of the ears. Principals punish swearing while wondering why their schools have racial problems.

The profane Big Seven (f^ck, sh!t, c*ck, c^nt, b!tch, b@stard, @ss) mark exclusively Eurocentric (and usually WASP) prohibitions. Words evolve from other words. In the case of the Big Seven, we encounter distillations of various European languages including Old Norse, Latin, French and Gaelic. Prohibiting these words artificially freezes them, heightens their national origins and impedes their inevitable migration and evolution. The three big contenders for the origin of our *f^ck*, the Latin *futuere* (to strike), the German *ficken* (to strike) and the Old Norse *fukja* (to drive), are, I admit, rarely glimpsed around our homes, schoolyards, locker rooms and factories. The continued prohibition of *f^ck*, however, constantly reminds us just who populates our ruling class. When our principals forbid words, they forbid cultures.

Canada is an independent culture, "strong and free."

Why, then, do we continue these antiquated European language prohibitions? How have oppression, denial, disingenuousness and naïveté become values we want to spend huge sums of money instilling in our children? We might laugh at past absurdities, such as Dr. J.S. Farmer's lawsuit to force his own publishers to print certain words in his pioneering *A Dictionary of Slang*. The fully evolved chuckle over Thomas Bowdler's 1818 *The Family Shakespeare*, in which "those words and expressions are omitted which cannot with propriety be read aloud in a family." The omission of *f^ck* from Harold Wentworth and Stuart Berg Flexner's 1963 *Dictionary of American Slang*, however, makes the book such a laughable failure that we are forced to admit the folly of quarantining a few words.

Our media overflow with rants about the dishonesty of today's leaders, yet our school principals forbid expression and demand blind adherence to unjustifiable rules. Chrétien's *Red Book* is full of sh!t, and we all bought it.

Schoolyard profanity does, of course, surround schoolyard problems such as aggression, racism and sexism, but these are problems of hatred, not word choice. Let's stop teaching a fraction of the language and blindly, destructively prohibiting the remainder. Jonathan Swift reminds us that "oaths are the children of fashion." Let's teach our children a little fashion sense.

— Russell Metz, Ph.D.

"What are you thinking?" Kim thrusts an open newspaper at Russell as she brushes past into the apartment.

"Morning, Kim. You look great."

"That'd be my fuckin' fashion sense. What are you doing?"

"Making a point. And coffee. Want some?"

"No you're not. Lots of milk if it's still that horrid continental."

Kim drops into a kitchen chair, tucking a foot under the opposite thigh. She wears the same sleeveless black shirt and sweeping bellbottoms as the café girls, but all in the crisp Dry Clean Only fabrics of the law office. Kicking off the other shoe, Kim makes no attempt to disguise her survey of the kitchen.

"Is it worth it, really worth it, Russell?" She takes the offered cup in both hands.

"Oh, rent's not bad. I'll be fine for —"

"Stop. Think you can give me a kiss without going to pieces?"

"Depends. Tongue?"

"Bastard."

She closes her eyes as they kiss dryly on the lips.

"He's thirteen. Things are going to really happen for him soon. Think of the stigma — parents, other teachers. I don't know whether your little rant will get him beat up by the schoolyard thugs or martyred."

"Hey, c'mon." Russell encircles her forearm with his hand. "Thugs don't read."

"This isn't a clever prank." Kim jerks her arm free and nods at the paper. "This could really hang over him."

"Going to lawyer lunches and lawyer parties, do you ever meet anyone with a passing interest in justice?"

"Don't start. Yeah, Russ, you're right. You really are. His principal's a prick in polyester, and a few intelligent readers will agree with you. But I just don't want him prejudged. Oh, Spenser Metz-Dawson, trouble."

"So he should plea bargain? Roll over for the lighter sentence?"

"It's not Milhaven."

"It's not right."

"It's public school."

"I'm sure fuck is equally forbidden at Middle Lake."

"Touché. I should go. You are right, and honest, but only the lonely and the strong like trouble."

Early the next morning Russell sits at the computer, glancing over the UBC English department web site. As Dr. Olde suggests in . . . I suspect I'm not alone in the belief that . . . The slowly changing web pages give him plenty of opportunity to glance repeatedly at a framed photograph of him and Kim sitting together in a huge fuzzy chair. Wrapping him from behind with both arms and legs, Kim smiles at the camera while pulling Russell's ear with her teeth. He just can't be single again, his dating skills are all pre-VCR, pre-E.

The front door opens. A familiar weight drops to the floor.

"Spense?"

"That's the one."

"You feeling okay?" Russell leaves the computer, follows the noises.

"Fine."

"So you're here because . . .?"

"Suspended." Spenser turns to the kitchen, practising his adolescent male gait and grimace of perpetual hunger.

"Whoa, hold the team. I'd like to hear what happened."

"I don't think Wellsley found your editorial very enlight-ening."

"You didn't do anything, there were no other —"

"Called down to his office first thing this morning. 'Your behaviour, as bad as it is, has come under additional attention. This behaviour cannot be valourized.'"

"What? I'll impale him. Valourize! Ugh. I'll burn him at the

21

stake. Spense, this isn't about you, not anymore, your principal's got problems he's taking out on you. I won't let him." Russell paces the kitchen, absently rubbing his stubble. "Save my files for me." He heads to his room to change.

"You going down to put him right, Hoss?"

The bathroom sink is filled.

"Plan on returning this afternoon."

"Aw, my soaps."

"He sees me *now*." Russell charges at the desk of the principal's flustered secretary.

"And you are . . .?"

"Loud and mean. Russell Metz, father of Spenser Metz-Dawson. You'll find him at the top of your list of the Gratuitously Punished."

"I'm afraid Principal Wellsley's in a meeting."

"Interrupt him. This is an emergency."

"He's with someone from the Board."

"Not anymore."

The secretary glances nervously towards the principal's closed door. Russell crosses to it and raises his knuckles to knock. "Which one of us announces me?"

"Principal Wellsley," she says into a speaker phone, "I'm sorry to interrupt, but Dr. Metz is here with an emergency."

"I'm coming out," a warbly voice replies. Wellsley tries to slip out casually, a pharmacist's palm already raised. His pale, corpulent flesh looks simultaneously antiseptic and germ-ridden.

Russell fires first. "Spenser comes back this afternoon. I'm not here to debate the lunacy, the cruelty of this suspension. Minimize your losses and take him back."

"Dr. Metz, this decision has been made."

"Hostile nations don't have to meet to remake it. Understand me clearly, Wellsley, I'm warning you. Don't punish me through my son."

"The school did not renew attention to Spenser's behaviour, but the school has to deal with the example it sets. Your belligerent tone —"

"I'm done talking. One last chance. He comes back at noon, or no amount of bake sales and Christmas pageants will save you from my exposure."

"The school will not be threatened."

"A silent death it is, then."

"City editor, please." Russell squirms out of his coat and glances around the apartment for Spenser, finding him on the couch. "Front seat," he whispers away from the phone, pointing towards the garage. "Yeah, hi. Russell Metz. You carried my Letter to the Editor this morning."

"The swearing guy, right?"

Spenser trails back and forth from the car with sheets of Bristol board, a shopping bag and a yardstick.

"You got it. Well, the plot's thickened. My son's now suspended, without having done anything else. I met with the principal. It's clear this is a hostage thing."

"That's too bad."

"Don't lose your perfectly healthy liver over it. I'm going to picket the school. 'University Instructor Lobbies for Swearing.' Need I mention my photogenicity? I'll be there in an hour." Hanging up, Russell dives into the fridge.

"You're going to picket the school?" Spenser hovers at the kitchen doorway.

"They've got a PR budget to rethink."

"So I'm not going back for one o'clock?"

"Afraid you're warming the bench for now. It'll be open arms tomorrow. Getting bored?"

"A little. Why don't I join you?"

"I don't want anyone blaming you. We can't have you walking around as the poster boy for corrupt youth."

"Oh, one of those all-right-for-you-not-all-right-for-me deals."

"Spense, I'm expendable here. Besides, think of the dates I'll score."

"I can already hear the panting rising up from the trailer parks."

"*Panting?* What have you been reading?"

"Free your mind."

"Lunch, then sign. I'm on a tight schedule."

"Nice work, my boy." Russell turns the sign from side to side.

"I was just labour. It's design I want." Spenser taps the end of a giant marker against his chin.

"You'll grow into it. Okay, where's my Discman, and tell me the batteries work."

"Easy, trooper. You're not out the door yet. What do you think you're wearing?"

"Good point. I'm already cast as the raging anarchist."

"Jeans out."

"A suit'd be too weird, might as well top myself off with a bowler hat."

"You're rationalizing your way to khakis and a jacket, aren't you?"

"Read me like a book."

Minutes later Russell pats down various pockets en route to the door.

Spenser approaches with one hand held behind his back. "Hey, you're forgetting the *pee* . . . uh . . . *pee-ay-sa* . . ."

"Pièce de résistance."

"That's the one." Spenser hands his father a dotted bow tie. "Now go get 'em. My day's all downhill from here."

Bow-tied, Russell hefts his sign and heads for the door, chanting one from the good old days: *Raise tuition? Not a chance! Let's burn a car like they do in France!*

"Hey Russ, you know I'm at Mom's for dinner, right?"

"Oh yeah." Russell taps a finger against his temple before pulling the door shut.

The Discman is invaluable. CBC omelet recipes save Russell from the sound of the laughter he can see in the faces of children behind classroom windows. Another set of curtains is whipped shut.

Strutting directly in front of the main doors, Russell knows the police are a possibility. It's a waiting game. After the papers, he'll gladly step off school property and wave his sign from the sidewalk. But the protest doesn't matter without a good photo.

Surely he'll get a warning before being charged with trespassing. One call to his lawyer. Very romantic.

How did people in the sixties survive the boredom of protesting? Oh yeah.

Profanity grows heavy on his shoulder. Weather updates crackle too frequently in his ears. A parting gold curtain catches his eye. Pale, pudgy arms slide a sheet of Bristol board between curtain and window.

"Wellsley!"

A thumb presses tape to the top of the sign, sealing it to the glass.

+ ONE

MORE

DAY

Prick! Thankfully a Chevette pulls into the lot and parks in a handicapped spot. Russell pockets his headphones.

"You Metz?" a tall man asks, stepping from the car and rummaging through the various pockets of his active-wear jacket and pants.

"You the cavalry?" Russell mimes photo-taking with his free hand.

"Just let me get my bugle."

"Look behind your left shoulder. There's our shot."

"One more day of what?" the photographer asks, unzipping bags, pouches.

"My son got suspended for saying fuck. I argued freedom of

speech, added a little protest. Now the principal's taking hostages, extending my son's punishment because I'm here."

"Mmm. Idiocy."

Russell does the full parade. Sign held high. One side, then the other. With flagpole in background. Beside a school signboard reading *Band sweatsh1rts going fast!!!*

"Okay, couple more in front of the principal's office. Perfect, keep looking above my shoulder. Do not move. Beautiful. Beautiful." Crossing to Russell, the photographer lowers his voice. "Look behind you. Our last little session here prompted him to take down his sign. I got *One More Day* getting swiped away behind your shoulder. You get your boy down here tomorrow and they turn him away, that'll go national."

Russell's eyes narrow. "You sneak too much porn as a kid?"

Russell slinks into the empty apartment, flopping down beside a phone. Divorce is a sour wind of change. Nibbled pencils become forensic relics. Each bedsheet is a pall. The phone doesn't sit, it taunts. He picks it up, dials.

"Hello, Duncan, Spenser there?"

"Yeah, sure thing, Geraldo." Duncan hands off the phone as footfalls approach.

"Hey Spense."

"Hey hero, you're on TV."

"Rains it pours. Listen, I wanted to tell you before your mom's shrieks spill the beans. I'm really sorry, Spense, but I think Wellsley has suspended you for another day."

"You think?"

"He did, I'm just not sure if he'll stick to it. I feel terrible that he's hurting you to get at me. He's wrong, several times over. I give up now, though, and he'll go on thinking he's right. Phone me anytime tonight or early tomorrow morning if you want me to change my mind, but unless you say no, I'm going back there tomorrow."

"No explanation?"

"The coward taped a sign up in his office window. A newspaper photographer got the whole thing."

"I didn't see it on TV."

"Imagine that. Makes you wonder whether it really happened."

"Well, you look pretty good."

"Yeah? How's the bow tie?"

"Buy a TV and find out."

"Nice try. I better talk to your mom. I love you, kid. I . . . I want you treated well."

"They call you a single father."

"That's nothing, you should hear what I get in the staff lounge these days."

"How do they find this stuff out?"

"Bribe the neighbours. We can egg Mrs. Burkes's house next time you're over."

"It's cheap, telling everybody your problems."

"Yeah, Spense, it is."

"Here's Mom."

Kim wipes her fingers before taking the phone.

"What are you doing, giving up academe for a ten-minute spot on *Canada AM*?"

"Justice, remember?"

"She's blind, not deaf. Nobody admits to liking the c-word."

"There was a time."

The fading sound of the television measures Kim's retreat from Spenser and their spacious living room. Russell hears a door close.

"I can only be so patient," Kim recommences.

"Wellsley's going to lose this. He's hanging himself."

"And Spenser along with him. We're slipping out early tomorrow afternoon, taking Spense to Montreal."

"Glad I could provide the long weekend."

"He needs stimulation."

"Watch the potty-mouth."

"Look, Wellsley's a joke. The whole school's rotten. We know that."

"I'm getting interviews. I'll find some money."

"Think so? After this?"

"We call it classroom energy."

"What's the UBC position?"

"Tenure-track."

"Jesus."

"There'll be others."

"You haven't lugged that brain of yours around all these years to teach at Mosquito College."

"I could get by here."

"Teaching Shakespeare to RMC cadets? You'd live off martinis."

"And Spenser would be in private school."

"He could be there now. Dunc's offered to pick up more of the mortgage. The fees won't kill us."

"How scorching. Your second husband will own our house so your flaky first husband's son can have an education."

"He's also willing to cover your half of the payments until you can pay him back."

"Great. I either have to admit he's a decent man or convince you he's doing it just to get into your pants."

"Up my skirt, you mean."

"Damn it, Kim."

"Yeah, well, that bow tie."

The waiting photographers, reporters and television crew are not the problem. Police at the gates are really no surprise. Condemning parents on the sidewalk are to be expected. It's the Men's Movement that has Russell groaning. A thin soldier in fatigues and beret keeps his small moustache level with the horizon, picketing like clockwork beside an overweight, unshaven man with granny glasses and extra copies of the *Socialist Worker* under his flabby arm. The male population of the nearest food court has volunteered for Russell's cause. A jowly man with stringy hair marches about in track pants and a shiny nylon jacket, broadcasting chronic unemployment and deluded rage with his sign: GOV'T HATES MEN. A fourth man appears dusty and misused, one of the walking wounded, with hair forever grey and an extra, dusty skin grown from his faded green work pants and shirt. He nods once at Russell. A sign rests against his shoulder: WHAT DID I DO?

Russell steps among them, praying the soldier doesn't salute and dreading the possibility of applause.

"Morning, fellas. Obviously I don't want to infringe on anyone's freedom of speech, but I have to be honest. Your sign," Russell inclines his forehead at Track Pants, "is counterproductive. It debases what we're trying to say here."

Naturally the soldier keeps quiet. The Socialist mumbles agreement. The Wounded Worker lights a thin, half-smoked cigar.

"Open your eyes —"

"We have, and we've seen the press, and we want to be taken seriously. A sign like yours has its place, in front of a courtroom for example. But here, in front of a school, we don't want to seem too" — partisan? strident? vitriolic? — "extreme."

"You got *cunt* on your sign!"

"Yes, well, people have seen my article. They know where I'm coming from."

"Reprinted again this morning," the Socialist informs.

"As if I'm marching without a sign."

"Well . . ."

"You gonna try and tell me I don't have a right to be here?"

"Wait." The Socialist leaps to action, digging through the pockets of his army surplus jacket and offering up a large black marker.

Track Pants rests his trotting high-cut sneakers for a minute, lowering the sign and leaning it against his doughy stomach.

Each of them stare at the words and letters.

"Don't hate men?" the Socialist suggests.

Russell begins his stroll, savouring his first free steps before they lock into an ellipsis of affected solidarity. His earphones are his only escape.

All afternoon, Wellsley's windows show only curtains.

The television crew returns. Russell slips off his earphones to catch *angry, custody* and *men* floating from the commentator's lips.

Around two-thirty, Russell spots a familiar Volvo at the school gates. Spenser steps out of the car and motions his dad over.

"Duncan need directions to Montreal?"

"Bagel money. You and the good ol' boys here are all over TV."

"Can I spin or what?"

"Yeah. Maybe you should quit while you're ahead, though."

"We're coming in on the kill."

"You've got an interview."

"It won't matter."

"Wellsley's not going to change his —"

"He'll have to."

"You look like one of them." Spenser juts his chin at the motley lobby.

"Sure, it's your call." Russell lowers the sign from his shoulder, rotates his elbow. "Risking a pinched nerve anyway."

"I just want it over, Dad."

"I understand, really. You could ask your mother about my overenthusiasm."

"I'm bored. It's just awkward."

"Hey —" Russell plays a few punches at Spenser's chest — "say no more, say no more. Well" — he looks up at the idling Volvo — "More-eeAL. Tell her to pick me up some beer."

"Do I get a carrying fee?"

"Parasite."

"I'll see you." Spenser trots to the car. "Wednesday," he calls back, head momentarily turned.

Russell winks back at him, tapping a finger against his temple.

Russell contemplates setting his answering machine on fire. Two messages await him.

"Hi, this is Lara Miller. I'm with CBC's *This Morning* —"

Russell punches the Forward key.

"Hey Dad, do me a favour." Spenser's voice crackles from a cellphone. "Put your sign up on my wall. The good side." A truck roars past. "See ya."

The machine clicks off.

Sitting Up

Danny shuts the half-open bathroom door to corner a fly. Buzz, buzz, still the black nugget buzzing. He reaches for a magazine. *Thwap!* The fly escapes upwards and buzzes along the white ceiling. *Thwap!* Danny stalks, a cylinder of *Popular Science* tight in hand. *Maclean's, Men's Health, Canadian Consumer*, a whole basket of them there in the corner — Dad Perry's reading room. Danny cringes at the phrase when friends are over. He got two good kick dents into the basket before anyone (Perry) said anything.

He's too annoyed to remember that the very science magazine he wields has been praising "Tomorrow's Soldier" from atop the tank for a week. *Thwap!* Danny steps onto the edge of the sparkling tub. *Thwap!* Grabs the shower curtain rod for balance. *Thwap!* Doesn't yet compare himself with the camouflaged soldier and his Game Boy gear. *Thwap! Thwap!* One, two, three before he falls.

"Danny, you okay in there?"

"Yeah, Dad. Just a" — *thwap!* — "fly."

Ruff. Ruff. Click. Click. Salsa the Collie Sheriff.

Thwap! Thwap!

Ruff. Ruff.

"What!"

"Fly, Dad, fly!" Danny gives it the old school try across the shiny white ceiling and down the tepid yellow walls. Minutes ago, when Danny was scalding his fingers under the tap, the door still partly ajar, Perry was off in a book.

"Oh."

Salsa's tags jangle and fade.

Thwap! The fly's body sticks to the slick paper. Danny knocks the corpse into the aquamarine garbage can and tosses the magazine on top of the rest.

"It's his third visit in less than an hour. Really." Rebecca's grip on her watering can tightens as she stares over at the man she has begun to think of as *her husband* more often than *Perry*. Her other hand repeatedly rolls and releases a clump of dead leaves. "What do we need, a signed confession?"

Perry looks up over his latest hardcover to fix her with a look both of them know he feels is beneath him.

"Privacy. Right to privacy."

The eczema's itch turned Danny's eyes back in his head. No longer able to see himself in the bathroom mirror, just chest, arms, thing on top of chest, Danny had been dousing his itchy fingers in scalding water. A knot of white light ties itself beautifully when he pushes the pulsing, weeping fingers forward into the cylinder of hot water. Lately he's been staring into the chrome faucet as the heat begins to chew too closely. He gives the last few seconds to this series of tiny distorted reflections, an entire rock band looming and head heavy in the bathroom video.

When he could see clearly again, he noticed the fly in the mirror. He didn't know if flies could hear, but he shut the door before turning off the tap just in case. His wet fingers dented the magazine as he rolled his baton. This one had been in the house for days.

Last Saturday Danny had walked back into his bedroom to the sight of a fly gumming his soiled blue Jockeys. Last Saturday, initiate in white knots, he'd jerked off for the ninth time and then gone to wash his hands.

His skin's been shot as long as he can remember. When he throws off the bedcovers, a blizzard of dust swirls in the strong morning sun. *Dyshydrosis*: patches of his young skin drier than any old man's, elephant elbows and dusty purple knees. *Eczema*: a rash he knows in every stage, the small white arrival, the red territorial ambition, the cursing yellow fade. And their passionate, incestuous affair: *dyshydrotic eczema*, a combination of scales and pustules on the fingers of his right hand, a series of fissures, flakes and swellings that arrive in under twenty-four hours and linger for as long as two weeks. But he's never had anything like this new frosty patch on his left thigh.

This past year, Rebecca has watched a claw come out. Fingers shield or hoard. No more hand gestures as he speaks. Eating and pointing with his left. Back in grades one and two, she couldn't imagine Danny caring at all. He would speak of his rash or his cream but otherwise be boy. He felt deprived only because he couldn't have bubble baths. And the scabs — other boys'd pick more.

Fly-killer Danny walks from the downstairs bathroom and passes the glowing living room and his news-hungry parents.

"'Bout time for bed, isn't it?"

"Going. Night."

His feet climb the stairs, but his hands, his inner hands, trace up and down F L Y.

On the couch, Rebecca's knees are in her hands. He's chair, feet up. Separate locations, blankets. Above her, Danny's sink starts going. Then the creak of the medicine cabinet. Squeak, squeak go the noise men.

This morning she brought it up with Perry.

"Bathroom. Bedroom. Car. Meet adolescence. Want another cappuccino?"

"No. I want to know what we're going to do about his sheets."

"C'mon. I get to use a power tool and blow bubbles in my milk at the same time."

Danny looks from the toothbrush in his left hand to his war-torn right. How does he get through the day? How can he actually get used to the pocked pink base, the cracks and lacerations that sediment like dry, flaked mud, the perpetual rainbow of infection? Rebecca has wiped chicken grease from her fingers and asked why he's bothering with a knife and fork. In this stage, everything seems to make them worse — writing, gloves, water, soap, the spit and toothpaste that run down a brush handle. He suspends handwashing, dreads every crap and reduces face washing to once a day. Masturbating? Skin rubbing skin? Good, it'll help him quit.

This time his fingers are so bad he washes his face with one hand, actually looking to his right elbow and imagining a stump. "Jim Abbott."

Danny looks up to Perry standing in the doorway.

"The one-handed pitcher I was telling you about. Plays for Philly." Perry smiles and nods at his son's hands.

"Thanks." Danny lowers for another rinse, angling to show Dad as much back as he can. He lingers with his face near the running water until Perry leaves.

Crossing his bedroom in darkness, Danny reaches for the light on his headboard. Plenty of light to read by, this he likes about his parents. In his underwear, he stares from his thigh into the mirror and back again. Nothing, just smooth skin. With a delicate fingertip he tries to locate some discernible edge to the patch on his thigh, to poke his way around the quicksand. Nothing.

The golf pencil he took from his mother's bag rests under the mattress. He writes evenly across the scarcely visible palm-sized patch as if his hip were the left side of a page and his knee the right. F L Y. The pencil leaves no mark. It's only the point he needs.

Lowering himself into bed, Danny swings the leg up as if it's locked in a cast. Carry that patch. Two years ago Peter Jenkins broke his leg and was showered with attention. Mrs. Billings let friends stay inside at recess with him and even permitted the occasional Jenkins obstacle course of desks and chairs. Sarah Miller gave Peter a whole box of wide markers to improve the autographs. By the next day Sarah and Renée had spent two whole lunch hours drawing up and down Peter. Danny had written *Sucks man* in squiggly blue ink and lost it all to a row of rainbow purple.

Danny pulls the bedcovers up slowly, careful not to disturb the thigh. Reaching for his book, he looks down one last time before lowering the sheets. He only dented the skin for the letters, kept every stroke clean. When he wakes in the morning F L Y will have risen in a neat, tough line of hives: *dermigraphia*'s the latest. Setting *Sword of Thieves* aside, he rolls a tube sock onto each hand and reaches for the light, waiting like a bird in the oven.

A clock and calendar of skin. His fingers are smooth and ordinary pink for a couple of weeks between each blitzkrieg of swelling and itching. Some try to ignore it. Others question (sympathetically or not) or offer advice — St. John's Oil, camomile tea and soap, nettles. The prescription creams, one stinking goop or another, can only keep the swelling and itching at bay. Healing happens or doesn't. Sailor boy Danny watches his skin, red at night, no delight.

All of this is trouble enough, and now these hives. At first he noticed them helplessly, dense and frozen in his skin like bubbles in ice. Every morning he'd stare down his smooth, fruit-skin chest to his treacherous thigh, back and forth in the wide mirror. Vanish. Vanish. Why here and not there? Why do his dad's whiskers grow only halfway up his face? One night Danny reached for a nearby pencil to poke for numbness or tenderness, just like the doctors. The next morning's hives weren't lines but dots, poke signatures.

Morning starts with a twenty tucked under Rebecca's list of questions for Dr. Schwartz. He keeps the money in his pocket all morning, occasionally scraping at its fine edge.

In the waiting room, he reaches for *People* and its assortment of low-cut dresses. He tries to keep focused on sequins and cleavage instead of the man across the room with a bubbly purple stain up half his face.

Sitting in front of Dr. Schwartz's large desk, Danny looks

past her and out the windows beyond. She murmurs a greeting while reading a file. The building across the street is almost identical to this one. Beside it another. Vertical blinds and fluorescent lights take up an overcast sky.

"Okay, Danny, let's see this leg."

Danny is motionless for just a second too long. Stupidly he reaches down to his ankles tugging at his pant leg to see if it will rise all the way up above his knee. Finally he stands and undoes the olive-coloured pants. The top of her desk is even with his young thigh. A pewter-framed family portrait stares at Danny's F L Y thigh, and the window measures his toadstool penis.

"Mm-hm. Hop up on the table behind you please, Danny."

Danny bends for his pants. How is she around that desk so quickly? She whacks his ass with her file folder. "Get used to it," she says, beating him to the table. One small dent of heat radiates from his butt over the table's crinkling paper. Soon enough she's at him with an illuminated magnifying glass. The other large but sloping hand comes down for stretch and pull. Her hip presses into his knee.

It thickens.

He hauls his folded arms in tighter. She plays at the hives with a dry cotton swab. *Salsa's been hit by a car. Salsa's been hit by a car.*

"Dermigraphia." And she's back to her desk.

Danny hops off the table, hauling his pants up before he hits the ground. Snapping the dome at his waist, he thinks again of how much he hates these pants, their sick, greenish hue, their stiff, scratchy feel. His penis subsides mercifully in pants his mother bought. Doc Schwartz taps a pen down the file.

"Any other patches like this one?"

"No."

"Has it gotten any bigger?"

Danny leaves with another topical antihistamine. The skin on his thigh has become a template of hives. Localized pressure, a thumbprint, say, or a thin medical instrument, becomes embossed in hives eight hours later. Traitors hide in his cells, awaiting just one command. Rise.

"Danny! What have you done to your leg?"

Rebecca practically drops the cereal bowl she had been reaching to set in front of him.

"Nothing."

"What do you mean, nothing?"

Rebecca pulls the leg of his Bermuda shorts up to reveal H A N D written in puffed-up hives. His friends all wear high-cut soccer shorts. She thought he'd want something longer.

"Excuse me," Danny snaps, brushing her hand aside. He shifts his chair and reaches for the Raisin Bran.

Her chin keeps going, and her lips form and reform a silent *P* as a lost commander shouts *Perry! Perry!* into the din. Turning with the gawkiness of an industrial crane, Rebecca looks down, conscious of her collarbones and the thinness of her nightgown.

"You cannot do that."

"Doesn't matter." He pretends to read the cereal box.

"You'll only make things worse."

"No I won't." He looks directly into her face. "Dr. Schwartz told me nothing will make it worse. It's from the inside. It just is."

"I don't want you doing this to yourself."

"I don't want lots of things done to me."

"Danny — that's disgusting."

"Exactly." He stares at her with a milky spoon in his left hand. She turns away.

Danny isn't aware of the steroids in his creams and doesn't realize track stars are impotent. The squat little pharmacy jars have evolved from dark brown glass to slick white plastic, and the typewritten labels have been replaced with laser-printed efficiency. Betamethazone, betanovate, cyclocort: more steroids than a football locker room, each one flung into a red sea. Learning the itchy time in his body, Danny is beginning to understand costs. Although the steroids usually reduce the swelling and ease the itching, they also thin the skin and suppress the local immune system. The tough fissures that end an outbreak are made susceptible to greater infection by the very substance that's supposed to help. The fingers torn raw by nails, cloth or scalding water now sediment and flake, the skin left weak and brittle by cortisone.

Occasionally Danny worries that the patches are actually the calibration of fear on his skin, as if the red advance up fingers and hands is the mercury in a thermometer of regret. It scares him. Not the pain or itching, not the lint-filled fissures or the candied yellow crystals that harden over the lesions, but the healing, the duplicity of a healthy hand. How to understand the light, whimsical departure? If one day is sickness and the next health, where, why does healing wait?

Danny flips through his robotics calendar, nervous of any Tuesday, wondering whether 28 August or, yikes, 2 October will be good or bad days. Turning back to July he studies his new thigh diary. 14 July: H A N D. 16 July: H E R. 17: H E R B. Reaching for his little pencil, he logs tonight's M A P in the perfect calendar square, studying it like a cautious engineer, a hopeful stage manager, a young coach.

"Dermimapia," he says out loud in the morning, showing Salsa a M A P of hives, an X on the spot.

Salsa doesn't lick Danny when his fingers are bad, and she's been walking slobber for years. Finally Rebecca read that licking, especially in female dogs, is an act of aggression. By then it was too late, old dog.

Locking his bike, Danny walks the few remaining blocks to the arcade. "Danny. Whassup?" Danny returns Ryan's greeting with a nod, hoping this not-too-close friend won't try a high five. It's that time of the cycle, and Danny is wearing long-sleeved shirts to the arcade, learning to take the summer heat and trying to ignore the sting of sweat in his open sores.

Dropping in his quarters, Danny starts up *Street Warrior*. High kick, low punch, shoulder throw. First go his sneakers, feet, legs. Nudge, nudge, half twirl into blip, pulse, groan. The redder his fingers, the higher the score. Roundhouse. Speedbag. Danny knows the distance between skin and bone. There is no time to scratch when he's ducking a simulated barrel or wielding a digital chain. Danny cracks a jaw and advances to the next stage, bathed in the machine's devoted glow.

Street Chick clips Danny repeatedly with a series of high kicks to the nose before Warlock buries both meaty fists in his kidneys. Danny catches the jump button with the mid-knuckle of his left hand, springing to a park bench before fully extending a leg into the base of Warlock's spine, earning extra points and increased speed.

Roused, Ryan shuffles over. "Bitchin." No one makes eye contact in arcades. Everything that matters is on-screen, even the reflections of their young, bursting heads. Danny never looks at his weeping fingers. A clear liquid, neither blood nor pus, shines up out of the rounder lesions. Mainline's coming at him with a broken bottle. Ratzo's got a baseball bat. Danny adds another quarter for extended life and watches his virtual chest heave. The longer he plays, the more he'll scratch when he's two steps outside.

Kicking up and down each member of the Stray Dogs, Danny steals a glance at Ryan's stadium face, wondering if this guy with better clothes and a four-hundred-dollar skateboard can see the mess on his fingers, the street-fighting glow reflected in small puddles.

Of course he shouldn't scratch. He's been doing it all his life on any surface he can find. The snug, severe edge of a rivet in the corner pocket of his jeans, good for a deft scrape in public. The tall worker of an open cupboard door. The mattress edge and its wobbly, giving abrasion. In cases of emergency, carpet. Dig on your knees.

Ryan doesn't say a word. Even if, against the odds, he admitted to admiring Danny's every kick and gouge, he's ultimately waiting for Danny to go down panting. Silence is the undisputed dialect of the arcade, respect and loathing slightly different gradations of a clenched jaw. Success in a game is only ever failure delayed.

Quick Dragon ends Danny with a flurry of punches up and down the mid-section before tossing his body onto the black spikes of a park fence and defiling it with pixelated spit. "Nice game," says Ryan, quarters in from the side. Still at the controls, Danny pretends to wipe his brow with one sleeve, surreptitiously patting his weeping fingers on the cloth he gathers. He enters DAN on the high-score list, then bangs away at the other buttons with Sleeve Two to mop up the tiny ichorous puddles they seem designed to hold. 59,345. Fourth place, not bad at all.

Walking out into the glaring sun, Danny already has a finger into a pocket to work the hard seam of denim. Stooping to unlock his bike, his face presses close to his thigh. The golf pencil is in the same busy pocket. 59,345 into the template skin.

Home around five, Danny slips in through the back. His parents' tense, combative voices stop him in his tracks.

"Only for the rough nights. Perry, he's ripping himself to shreds."

"Another drug?"

They're in the living room. Just past the hall.

"I'm only talking about a few nights."

"And what if they work? Then a few nights become nearly every night. The depressants weaken his immune system further and he's susceptible to more infection. Okay then, more antibiotics! Up, down. Up, down."

"He's suffering."

"No pill is going to change that."

Ruff! Salsa, aroused by the rising voices, begins circling rooms and spots Danny at the kitchen door. Danny reopens the door quickly and quietly, then shuts it again loudly.

"Hey guys!"

Salsa sinks her skull down to lean her long nose forward. Danny uses the clean thumb to work behind one ear.

Perry pops across the kitchen to herd Danny back to the door. "I didn't get a chance to walk Sals. Think you could give her a quick one?" Perry tugs at Salsa's other ear. The dog's skull ferries across a few inches of love. To one side of Danny is hallway, living room and his mother rotating potted plants. To the other, the kitchen counter and a box labelled Sleep-e-Deez.

"I'll get you an apple," Perry adds as Danny returns to the door.

Looking back at the tossed apple, Danny notices the counter swept clean.

Staring down at a sizzling skillet, Rebecca stands as if split open, each rack of ribs a shutter hanging loose off her spine. Fresh air and Danny enter with the dog. A hissing network of onions stirs beneath her spatula. In the chrome kettle, she sees his back fade behind hers. Hot oil leaps regularly from skillet to chrome. She can stand above him, yelling every protest or threat, and still he'll peel one finger with another. She used to pull his wrists apart and stop him with a square look in the eye. Glancing through his books while cleaning up his room, she has seen small yellow stains on the pages. And the magazines under his mattress. She can see the rash on his hands from across a room and knows he dreams of stroking, of burying those fingers.

The potatoes are nearly done. Perry and Danny are talking in front of the TV. He can stop Danny's scratching with two low words from the back of his throat or a hand around each wrist. Hey fella. Stop it. It's the same voice Salsa never disobeys. Rebecca hates the way he can split the name like firewood. Sal-sa.

The meal is hard, silent, one fork after another. She's relieved to get up for another bag of milk. Danny doesn't stay for ice cream.

Silently removing a cold pack from the freezer, Danny heads up to his room. He lays the cold, pliant plastic over the day's fading score and reads to pass the time. Cold to bring down the hives. Eventually he lays a dirty T-shirt between thigh and liquid ice. After an hour, it's Rebecca's hair dryer.

This time he's slow with the pencil, stretching out the three letters to their maximum height. He uses the dryer all evening to accelerate the hives. The TV muted, Perry eventually yells up about the noise.

"Just trying to get some glue to dry."

"What's that?"

"Surprise."

And the TV floods again.

Danny wakes late, his dad already gone and the sun shining for a dozen Julys. With crazy hair and the smell of sleep all over him, Danny hunts out his mother at the dining room table. Bathrobe. Open newspaper. Mug of coffee.

Having thrown on just his shorts, Danny flinches slightly with the morning chill. "Mom, look," he says, raising the shorts up his thigh for M O M.

She cries like he's never heard. Her chin goes to rubber and the tears stream onto her peach bathrobe there in the morning sun. Steam rises from her coffee. Danny sees *old*, sees *lonely*.

A Sharp Tooth in the Fur

Sure, buying a pair of black panties would have been more convenient than stealing Rachelle's, but Dean's never found any fucking in *convenient.*

Starting out does take time. Looking for work is work. That some of his friends have found good jobs is inevitable, what with their weak grades, anemic vocabularies and absolute inability to think independently. Just because Rachelle dumped him after two years around the same time she started bringing home seventy-plus doesn't necessarily mean she's superficial, materialistic and self-centred.

"Do you think I'm going to work at the Information for the rest of my life, that film and anthro are the perfect preparations for another draft, buddy? I don't. There are moments when I'm afraid, and I'm sure as hell frustrated most of the time, but I don't really believe bartending is my fate. Sounds like I'm alone in that opinion."

They haven't even spoken in a month, and technically Dean's returning to Rachelle's apartment as Natalie's date. Well, returning to her at least. The apartment's new. No, not returning *to* her. Near her. Tonight's the house warming.

New to the turf, invitation uncertain and sharing a doorway with Natalie, Dean nonetheless struts in like an exiled crown prince. *Moi, moi,* he kisses at Rachelle across the crowded room, one pucker for each glacier cheek. Drop the girl, gain a drink, case the joint. New Japanese knives. The kilim, their kilim, now a wall hanging.

One-time author of an "elegant, rivetting" undergraduate thesis on filmic cross-cutting and shamanistic dream voyages and now a master of "real limey" margaritas, Dean divides life into busywork and doubt. High priest of doubt, he meets busy workers Jen, and Jen and Jen, each of them a synergy motivation consultant. *Heads up* caroms around the room like a ball. *Heads up* as a thing. Reluctantly working in a bar dispels any hope that three quick glasses of wine might be the antidote to convergence-this and signing-off-that. A bedroom, that's an antidote.

Darker of course, and cooler. Even in this half-light the Yves Klein monochrome above the bed is a jolt of pure, blue energy. Dive into the electric blue. Be a nuclear seal.

Not finding any bedside reading to disapprove of, he's quickly over to the high, faux art nouveau dresser. Double curled handles. Curvaceous blond inlays. The top drawer pulls out slowly to avoid a single squeak. The dim light and careful pace reveal only a centimetre at a time. Blacks huddle and hide in the deep, wide shadow. More and more drawer must open to dissolve the bumpy mass into matte cotton and iridescent silk, discernible lace, tiny clasps and gauzy stockings. The Klein blue buzzes along with the electricity in his testicles as black, crimson, indigo, ivory and white become high-riders, low triangles, wide bras, thin cups, knee-high socks and endless tights. His fingers trace the wood first, up the side, straight and hard, before diving into cotton, silk, silk. A finger hooks the thinnest of hip straps and tugs one little bundle free from its neighbours. He is reaching in with the other hand when he spots Rachelle standing in the doorway.

One of the seven Canadian men who didn't grow up playing hockey, and living in a country without national service, Dean has grown into adulthood little bloodied and little bloodying. Violence for Dean is much like economics, entirely theoretical and rarely interesting. Seeing Rachelle with arms crossed, and with one of her black waistbands stretched between his fingers, Dean is either thinking violently or simply picturing Clint Eastwood.

In his grandfather Western, Eastwood walks into the saloon to take on an entire posse and wins with a toss, not a gun. Every hired hand in the place is shocked when Eastwood's rifle appears to jam. That fake jam is Move One. Move Two is the clincher. Eastwood tosses the apparently faulty rifle at the first line, who, flash men of dexterity and bravado that they are, reach to snatch the Winchester from the air. Move Three is the crouch and pistol work that levels the full-handed men and their blocked compadres. Eastwood slaps that hammer and Dean tosses the panties at Rachelle. Watching their black arc, he comes up with two options. If she steps to avoid the expensive missile, he'll start joking and apologizing his way to one dollop of shame square on the chin. If she lets them hit her, he'll reach for a handful of thigh. Rachelle has a third idea.

Stepping forward, she catches the panties in mid-air with her teeth. Frisbee dog, she shakes black in her triumphant mouth. "Gee, Dean, I missed you, too."

To soften the belief that we control our bodies, young stage actors are often coached to cross a stage by imagining they are getting tugged ever so gently by an invisible string tied to their belly buttons. Dean crosses to Rachelle on a navel string of intuition to grab the black in her face.

"I need to borrow these."

"Couldn't you just download something?" she asks through clenched, tugging teeth.

"No, really, it's a different kind of experiment."

"Girls' panties. Whoopee cushion. Maybe a wig?" Suddenly she yields her catch. "You're not making another film, are you?"

"Have you ever seen someone choked to death with her gold card?"

"Okay, Dean, sneak the goods." She throws just a sliver of ass into her exit walk. "You'll wash them — by hand — when you're done."

Sadly, disastrously, affair sex is usually great. One-sided, two-sided, the first, the second, the third time. Make-up sex has just the right mix of attention and revenge. Second-language sex — amazing to see where the humour comes out. Although usually high in alcohol, proximity sex (housemates, best friends of siblings, co-workers) is notably voracious. Fresh-divorce sex competes strenuously for lost time. But is there better sex than post-break-up sex? Knowledge does not get packed away with the photos and trinkets. Lust doesn't believe you can never go home again.

Dean tries to keep the sex ghosts at bay while walking between shops. Opening the door to Rose and Thorn Lingerie, he heads straight to the sales counter. "As strange as this might appear, I don't want to seem like I'm shopping with my pockets." He reaches into the breast pocket of his jacket for Rachelle's undies. "I've got a new friend, so I've brought something along. Size can be such a . . . thorny issue. What do you recommend?"

Although nothing special, a black blazer from Kensington, the jacket is crucial. He can't just pull a ball of underwear out of his jeans. No, inner jacket pocket, undies folded once like a construction paper valentine. It's just after five p.m. He still has to hit Agent Provocateur, Second Skin and Just Black before taking over a shift at eight.

"The Information."
    "My, what a commanding phone voice you have."
    "Born spy."
    "Okay, Bond, when do I get the gear back?"
    "They're not exactly your only option."
    "Glad to hear you got through the whole drawer. Maybe they're my lucky pair."
    "I'm sorry, do you need luck these days?"
    "What is it that sharpens the rapier wit, cutting the lemons or short-changing Debbie the waitress?"
    "Counting other people's money before I sleep. All right if I bring them back late Sunday afternoon?"
    "Any chance you'll bring an explanation?"
    "I thought you might prefer the shroud of mystery."

"Hello again," Dean begins at Rose and Thorn. "I was in for these Friday night. Turns out . . . well, let's just say they won't be needed anymore. I have the receipt." The Rose, Agent, JB, Skin. Heather (920-0528), nothing, nothing, Michelle (869-5255).

When Dean first read Milan Kundera's suggestion that men want beautiful women whereas women want men who have had beautiful women, he thought, Milan, you dog. Old world dog. Months later, in the trickling wisdom that closed a fight between him and Rachelle, though, she made a bridge back to politely sexist Milan.

"In your elementary school, when you saw two boys fight, what did it look like?"

"Circle of kids around two guys bloodying each other's noses."

"And what did it look like when two girls fought?"

"We weren't a pay-per-view school, so I didn't get much girl on girl."

"Uh-uh. It's never girl on girl. It's girls on girl. Democratic hate. Sally cross you? Or, more simply, Sally looking weak? Turn Lisa against Sally. Mary — who likes Lisa but isn't liked much by her — will phone you within a day and a half. Pretty soon Sally's friends are going to have to decide where they stand in the new world order. It works precisely because next month it's going to be somebody else on the outside, quite probably you."

"If I'd listened more carefully, would I have learned all of this in the skipping songs? Rich man, poor man. Divide. Conquer. Crush?"

"You're pimping my panties."

"I'd say bluffing. They're a prop. You make it sound like I'm touring construction sites at lunchtime."

"Well, what did you think I'd make of your little show and tell?"

"Frankly, I can't see the problem."

"Stacey saw you. If you're wondering."

"Stacey saw me what?"

"Your little trade-up-the-ladder number."

"Yeah, what did she sound like as she told you?"

"Pig."

"Listen. That little black Faria sweater I gave you, do you only wear it around the house now because it wouldn't feel right to go out looking hot in something I gave you? I thought not. Same principle."

"C'mon Dean, there are no principles in panties."

"If you think about it," Rachelle begins her next call, "there's nothing pant-like about them. I'm assuming that's how it works, like booties for tiny, softer boots. Back in the days of knee-length bloomers I could see it: pants, panties. But now — the focused V, the hip-hugging triangle — shouldn't we move on?"

"Not much pant in a thong."

"So this stunt of yours worked, did it?"

"Suppose that depends on what point we call it working, but yeah, it paid off."

"Well, why not go with the real thing next time?"

"Wouldn't you miss it if I borrowed your ass for a few days?"

"Let's go shopping tomorrow night. Your credit card, my me. Return the stuff later with your broken man bit and see how you do."

"Uh, yeah, okay —"

"Panty got your tongue?"

"For a minute. Stop by for a drink around six-thirty."

"If I'm in the neighbourhood feeling a little daffy, sure."

The drum 'n' bass loops. The snaking lights. The ostentatious porn.

Dean has barely seated himself in the low-slung leopard-skin chair when Rachelle returns from the change room. Barefoot and already down to one of her thinner undershirts, Rachelle steps past the attendant Monique and the helpful Denise. She drops her cellphone into Dean's lap and then turns on an ad-lib dime.

The refundable prostitution. The germ money. The fluor-escent love.

Rachelle arrived in a kinderwhore/vamp fusion of midriff and mascara. A triangle emerged in seconds, with Monique and Denise all but throwing aside their take-out cappuccinos to conspire, compete and compliment. Rachelle's "I'm looking for something a little more swishy" was the secret password of fashion. Out came the black. The parade of svelte Tachtel, astro-naut glitter and gauzy polyamids began. Cling and flow. Drop and rise. Watching Rachelle strut back to the change room, Dean would gladly hold onto a live grenade so long as he could watch the apple music of her ass.

The thongs. The VPLs. The nothings.

Breastless fifth wheel that he is, Dean goes on the attack. "Wool and nylon? Those blacks together, no. Too beachy for socks."

Who is this guy tacking back the corners of the chair with his shoulders? Did the back hinge of his jaw always move like that when he spoke? Sensing Monique and Denise's fickle turn towards Dean, Rachelle stoops to folding up her hair in both hands. "Yeah, that's it," he practically yells. She's forced to tug at her bra to steal back a little fire. Back in the change room, she jerks nobody's pants down with both thumbs.

At the checkout, Monique and Denise smile their lip-gloss smiles, Dean has swallowed the canary, and Rachelle is forced to lash.

"Aren't you going to phone us a cab?" she asks public-trans-port Dean.

"Sure." He digs her phone out of his jacket. "Do you have a number?"

"Oh, whomever you normally use."

She can see his eyes tighten, can't they?

"I'll call you a cab." Monique tears herself away from fluffing and refluffing the top layer of tissue paper.

Stepping out onto the sidewalk, Dean says, "Why don't I buy you a drink before we decide what's next?"

"This is my idea as much as it is yours. Let's just go. FX it is."

Rachelle refusing alcohol is never a good sign. "I didn't say it wasn't your idea. I asked you if you wanted a drink."

"Actually you said, 'Why don't I buy you a drink?' which is more like asking me if you can ask me if I want a drink."

"Okay, fuck the drink. Let's hustle our way to happiness."

"Fine."

The F-word. He'd bitten his tongue to avoid saying it and now wishes he'd been the one to let fly. He considers pinching one of her long, creamy triceps but is saved by the arrival of the cab. "Well then, until we drop."

The driver's posted ID gives Dean an idea. "How about fake names? Nadya? Or Cassandra? Alias, alter ego, take your pick."

"Okay." Finally her eyes are as bright as her lips. "I want Bowie."

"Perfect."

"And what about you, old Smuggs?"

"Me, I should have grown a little shit-sucking moustache."

Outside FX Dean pays the cab and then hurries on ahead, muttering, "Play along with Chad," without giving her a chance to reply. Inside they telepathically synchronize their runway struts. Don't clench your jaw. No, open your spine, your ribs, until your skull feels like a crown. Let your jaw fall. Wear your power.

Terrifically arrogant shop girls soon flank Rachelle on both sides while Dean slaps down onto a cherry-red inflatable chair. Just before Rachelle reaches the corrugated iron change rooms, he asks, "How many times did Chad come shopping?" He waits

until her second trip — no, no, try the hooded one — before surreptitiously phoning a friend and asking him to call right back.

"Can you get that?" Bowie calls out.

"Sure." Dean's face hardens instantly, and he tosses the phone
at a startled lady-in-waiting. "Tell her it's Chad."

"Chad" opens the change room faster than a nervous skunk.
Flushed, Rachelle emerges in one shoe and the under-layer of a
two-piece dress. The clerks find sweaters to refold as Rachelle
approaches, chesty and apologetic.

"I said two words to him: It's over."

"Useful words."

"So long as there's trust."

Biting his cheek to avoid laughing, Dean watches her cream
turn, her purring walk. It's amazing she doesn't implode. Perhaps
spontaneous combustion starts with swishing hips and plump,
dove breasts. He floats, an erection stranded on the trapped air
of an inflatable plastic chair.

When they do fuck — stepping over wine glasses and bottles,
sweeping shopping bags off the bed with a blind backhand —
Rachelle looks every bit at home in a Caetano shoulder sweater,
and Dean wonders how much wine it will take the next time. Her
asking him to open a second bottle, had it been fun or insulting?
Dean the tattoo needle. His hand, his fist reaches for the sweater.

And soon there are no questions. Hair. Skin. The long play
and dive. His cornerstone hip. Her cow-tongue feet. Coaxing him
onto his stomach, riding his tailbone, she erases the months
they've been apart. Holding her by one wrist, he knuckles the
spot at the base of her neck. She coos at every tug and scratch of
the sweater. Avoiding the dangling, cardboard tags and plastic
loops would be far too cautious. No, each tag is a tiny, hidden

pang, a tooth in the soft fabric fur. One, two bites across the high plains of her chest. Twice up each candescent thigh. Reaching into another bag, then up her dress, Dean uses both hands to saw a camisole through her crotch. Naturally the camisole is rubbed over his whiskers, wrapped around his neck, balled into his kidnapped mouth. Then the flailing. His back. Her thighs. All clothes off, the sawtooth camisole is the tiny black she squirms into as they slide Dean in. The straps he tears down.

"I guess this one's a keeper," he finally says, tugging her camisole stomach as they sink into damp pillows.

"Ooooh, the pampering."

"Don't let it go to your head."

"Or what, next week I'm demoted to Le Château? One more peep out of me, young lady, and it's Smart Set for good?"

Finally he can just smile, wrap both shoulders and smile.

Accepting the coloured rope handles of various bags in the late morning sun, Dean says, "Feels like custody."

"At least it feels like something."

He doesn't kiss her and he doesn't walk away quickly enough and there's next Saturday, Saturday.

Non-Violent, Not OK

Around midday (he'd decided against a watch), Chuck saw the march from the belly of a giant pig. Sometime after four he was squirting diluted Maalox into the twice milky-eyes of a blind man. "You're stronger than the gas," he heard himself say. "You're stronger than the gas," pumping dumb out of his pamphlet mouth.

Several weeks earlier Chuck's phone was beside him on the couch, so he actually did reach for it.

"Charles. Good. Listen . . . uh, nobody's dying, and I haven't done anything to your mother, but get a hold onto something because, well, I'm declaring bankruptcy. I'm broke."

"What?"

"Bankruptcy. I'm skewered. Poor in Armani sweaters."

"How?"

"*Spent* and *have* aren't quite matching up."

"What about your connections?"

"Connections, especially political ones, are all dogs. They know the smell of blood. And buddy, I reek."

"What does this mean?"

"I guess you grow up after all."

"Share the ad with your neighbour and tell us what you see."

Professor Sinclair gave Chuck his one-browed *You're late* but refused to let go of a good roll.

"This isn't a trap. Just verbalize what you see. What kind of object is it? An alarm clock, right. See how easy this is? Very quotidian. What assumptions does this clock make? No, John, not 'Time exists.' Simple assumptions. What two main functions does the clock perform? Forget about its soup-can radio. Tells the time, yes. Wakes people up, there we are. What kind of people does it wake up? We've got — Sarah — exactly: His and Hers alarms. Not Alarm One and Alarm Two. His and Hers. According to this monkey-shit brown alarm clock, beds are shared by a man and a woman, not by a man and a man, not by a woman and a woman. His and Hers. This is power. True power is invisible. Invisibility is the power of power. Ten days from now, when the RCMP start a-clubbin' in Quebec City, that's only the tip of the iceberg. My pay stub's a better manifestation of power. I look at my pay stub, and I see that I'm *paying* the RCMP to beat me. See you next week."

"Affinity Groups. Spokes Councils. Art and Resistance. That should be enough for tonight."

Chuck looked around the common room, relieved that dreadlocks and unravelling second-hand clothes weren't absolutely mandatory. Deodorant and razor blades obviously didn't see much of the protester set, but, physically at least, he might just pass. (Mental note: more hemp jewellery.) Surprised to have come and surprised not to be turned away, Chuck concentrated on not blowing the Audible Capital Letters.

"Kir, you want to start us off with Affinity Groups?"

"Yeah, but won't that take me right into Spokes Councils? Do you want to come in at the end of that, Dave? Great. Let's start with the Grid."

Hairy people without shoes began laying masking tape onto the blue carpet to form hasty letters.

V OK	V N OK
N V OK	N V N OK

"The people you like to go for beers with are not the same people you should go into Confrontation with in Quebec. You must be part of a unit to be strong, and these units will break apart if the members don't share the same attitudes about Direct Action. Let's all step over to the Grid and run through a couple of Scenarios."

This wasn't so bad, Twister for revolutionaries.

"In my top — which is it again? — left, we have 'Violent but I'm OK with it.' Next on the right is 'Violent but I'm Not OK with it.' Bottom left it's 'Non-Violent and I'm OK with it,' then 'Non-Violent, Not OK.' Let's say we're walking down one of the march streets and someone shatters a McDonald's window. Find your place on the Grid. Do you think breaking the window is violent or not, and is that OK with you?"

Chuck shuffled with the big group into Violent and OK. A smaller crowd assembled in the Violent and Not OK square, leaving Kir free to strut between the bottom quadrants.

"Why do you think it's violent, and what makes you OK with that?" Kir pointed at someone far too close to Chuck.

Chuck panicked as he tried to think of a slogan, of anything. What did any of this mean? What's Non-Violent and I'm Not OK with it? What is that?

Fortunately, his neighbour had a crowd-pleasing answer. "They're fucking McDonald's."

Laughter rippled through the dense crowd. Shoulders, especially Chuck's, jerked up and down.

Until now Chuck could stand in a kitchen (in his hiking boots) and let a pot boil over, accurately arguing "It wasn't mine," if pressed and suffering no risk of contradiction because he never cooked for himself. If your girlfriend dumped you, insulting everything about you including your friends, Chuck wouldn't wait an hour before asking what, exactly, she had said about him. He had too many jeans and paid a laundromat to wash them. That knit-eyebrow look female classmates gave him went right on by, that determined effort to fuse his smug lips.

Toys, trips, clothes, computers — Chuck learned to counterfeit the word *need* when Henry, his dad, moved out of their house and into his cellphone. I need a tent and some stuff for Labour Day weekend. For the moguls, it's gotta be the new Salomons. A portable CD player with *better* memory. Not until the next September, when Chuck moved with what remained of his expensive things into a low-ceilinged, blue-carpeted student hovel paid for with loans, did he realize that he could think of almost no thing that was his father's. Certainly not a house. The phones changed more often than the cars. Disposable coffee cups, natch. The camera was always someone else's, here's a twenty, send me a set of doubles. If Henry flew Chuck to meet him for a week of skiing, Henry had gear. Should Chuck happen to meet his dad in an apartment or a suite or at Mary's or Susan's, there'd be no skis, no fishing rods, no bike. Wait, his luggage. Henry definitely had luggage.

Despite his nervousness, Chuck was relieved his dad's phone still worked.

"Dad, I'm going to go —"

"Right, Chuck, listen. Put anything you need on the Am-Ex, and I mean yesterday. Go get groceries, buy in bulk. Get clothes. Pester your dentist for a cancellation appointment. Take out only, don't risk a sit-down meal."

"Dad, I'm going to Quebec City on the twentieth."

"You can't visit while —"

"I'm not visiting. I'm protesting the Free Trade Area —"

"What about it?"

"Well, corporations can force us to accept chemicals or drugs we don't feel are safe."

"You're worried about safety, so you're going to the largest assembly of riot police in Canadian history? Slow down, Chuck. What's it going to solve if your skull gets cracked?"

"If we don't protest now, it'll be too late."

"Says who? It's never too late to keep your head in one piece. Start smaller. Go to local protests. Write your MP. Don't dive into the deep end."

"I'm going."

"That's not going to be easy on your mother."

"Dad, nice one."

"I need to defer my exam so I can go to the FTAA protests in Quebec."

"Sit down, Chuck, sit down." Professor Sinclair rolled his chair away from his desk and turned toward Chuck. Though narrow, a tall window let enough light past a few spindly plants to flood the floor beneath their feet. Only at this time of day, at this moment of Chuck's stroll-by meeting, could this seem like an office of sunlight and not an office of books.

"We can do that, right? Defer the exam for Quebec?"

"You can do anything. That's done. You go. We trust you're there. You write when you get back. I'm surprised, though" — Chuck saw every inch of Sinclair's slow stretch back in his chair — "pleasantly surprised that the administration went for our proposal. Let's hope other ears are as attentive. So what takes you to Quebec?"

"Well, the whole thing, really."

"The fence?"

"That's crazy."

"Democracy for the rich."

"And, uh, now there are bylaws forbidding scarves around your face."

"Oh, they've been quashed already."

"Well, still."

"Yeah. And hey, Chapter Thirteen."

"I know. I can't believe that."

"Issues as important as the legality and safety of industrial chemicals will be decided by closed council and not by government. Is this possible?"

"Where are the people?"

Only when Sinclair leaned all the way forward did Chuck stop nodding his head. For a moment, Sinclair just looked at him from a box of sunlight.

"Take that question with you, Chuck. I doubt you could name a single FTAA proposal, and I don't care. Chapter Thirteen, Chapter Eleven, MMT, whatever. You've never once *had* to write my exam, have you?"

Names and phone numbers had been written and rewritten on loose-leaf paper. Buses actually got chartered. Pooling with another university three hours distant (Henry would approve), students could make the round trip for thirty-five dollars.

Waiting for the ambitiously late bus, Chuck stood in one spot, then another as day turned to cool night. These — what? comrades? — looked more like Phish fans than social agitators. Surrounded by body piercing and expensive camping gear, Chuck hoped the police didn't have magnets and saw the reach of other paying dads. Only one guy had a sign (SHARE, just SHARE), and it was an obvious pain to carry, hold or load.

Quickly enough, though, the bus had its own highway glow. A scraggle-bearded guy across from Chuck took bus money, scrunching bills into his crowded fist and scratching at a crumpled sheet of paper stretched across one thigh. He was a classmate who didn't show, a Frisbee guy, and suddenly he was playing accountant while rowing metal down the night to stop child labour and pesticide expansion and rule by the few. A chartered bus full of protesters, canned democracy laced with hockey-team spirit. Chuck could see two people reading talking-pig Orwell. A couple snuggled under a blanket. A woman in her fifties wore good walking shoes and passed around bags of dried fruit. A clipboard guy straight from the teacher's college assembly line leaned over the back of Chuck's seat to hand him a tube of silicone. "Plug any ports on your goggles and pass it on."

Violent and OK, he gets. He eats burgers. But what about the cold dissatisfaction of Non-Violent and Not OK? Damn this peace. Has history ever changed without this mode?

Road signs were not needed to tell them they were approaching Quebec City. Police cars began to slow and tail the bus. They just made it to the college where they would sleep before it closed. A proudly irresponsible kid who looked like he wore his pyjamas all day long tried to whine his way past volunteer door monitors impatient with this, his third lost entrance card in two days.

Walking up to one of the second-floor classrooms-cum-bunk-rooms assigned to their bus, Chuck noticed two things. Handbills were posted everywhere advertising a recurrent workshop: How to Speak to the Media. Climbing the metal stairs of a still escalator, he also thought of what an easy target they'd make. Shut off the escalator power from a locked cabinet in a distant part of the building, shut off speed and routine, and they were just sleepy kids with expensive knapsacks hiking single file up a narrow metal staircase.

Sun and singing and drums. Tens of thousands of protesters flooded the train station and port of Quebec's old city. The people were so thick it took hours to move from one end of the compound to the street. Throughout this marching city, duct tape, bungee cords and knapsack straps lashed bongos, water jugs and the occasional real drum around skinny chests. Ecstatic corduroy dancers swarmed the drummers. Chants rose and fell, blowing over the tectonic plates of bodies. *FTdoubleA, it ain't gonna stay. Avec nous, dans la rue. Avec nous.* Whistles pierced the warming air. The monotone voices of union leaders squeezed out of rented megaphones to rally troops in bulging denim and raise the lines of professionally printed signs. The talk and cry of forty, fifty, sixty thousand people vibrated somewhere between a purr and a growl.

Capes, scarves, banners, pinwheels, a few skateboards — gear to defend, gear to amuse. In fear of gas, the pimply trench-coat set preferred to go all the way back to World War I for the full elephant canister, while others wore nothing more than a painter's dust mask or the vented ski goggles even Chuck knew to avoid. The hippies were out with their paunches, canes and white beards, strolling with death in the afternoon. Here, pre-police, collars were open and sleeves rolled up in the sun. The full revolutionaries had phone numbers (Legal Aid? an Unarrestable?) written down their scrawny forearms.

The river of bodies flooded a wide street. Blond plywood covered most of the shop windows, and graffiti most of it. Louder cheers announced a hot spot in the landscape of noise. Two guys in coveralls climbed atop a van to work the two moving halves of an elaborately painted cardboard sign. A stars-and-stripes cock-and-balls pumped a pair of green planet buns over and over again.

Hey, Dad, it's not so bad.

A slow block or two later a whistle code cut through the hoopla. Squat women in dyed pink shirts and fatigues rushed past Chuck to congregate and cheer on a patch of sidewalk. *Ooh, uh-huh, uh-huh, uh-huh,* the guerrilla cheerleaders began their choreographed excoriations. *While you're eating your Wheaties* (one hand spooned cereal from the bowl of the other) *and beating your wienies* (both hands worked a python erection), *can you hear the crash of trees* (one hand cupped to the ear) *or a child worker say please?* (hands knitted together). The crowd hooted and clapped in this brief world where the fat girls could finally be cheerleaders.

Over and over again a set of drums would start up one of those songs by Paul Simon and some African guys nobody can name. *Du-du-du-dah, du-du-du-dah.* Three women beside Chuck struggled with a giant papier mâché pig. "Would you like to wear our pig?" Sure. With his head lost in the chicken-wire frame, Chuck felt along the pink sides to the stumpy stuffed-pantyhose legs and waved them at the crowd. Laughs to the right. Cheers to the left. Wiggle that rump.

"I think you're a born pig," one of the women said, sweat on her brow from her time in the belly.

"Oui, j'suis le cochon. Charles le cochon."

"Bonjour, Charles, je m'appelle Julie."

"Julie." Because of the noise and the sealed sides of the pig, anything he really wanted to say required him to slow to a near stop, risking collision from behind. He inclined a complete side of pork towards her, all the while hoping she would turn up to his chicken-wire face. "How do I say 'tear gas' in French?"

"Lacrymogène. La-cree-moh-jen."

He nodded gratefully *en porc*. Suddenly he thought of telling her about Sinclair. Lachrymose poets, he'd once said, and, breaking character, he'd defined it for them. Woeful. Tearful. Chuck had mentally rewritten the phrase as *cry-baby poets* and thus actually learned a new word. But what would he tell Julie about Sinclair, that maybe his complaints to his mom or his housemates or anyone who would listen meant something, that, wow, here was this distant hard-ass alongside him on the street? He reached out for Julie's hand and that of another pig girl from the other side and guided each small hand up to the nylon stumps that swayed unseen beside his caged ears, holding, just for a second, two warm hands in the spring sunshine.

The cries and chants bumped up against something and stopped. Peering out the pig periscope, Chuck couldn't quite see the trouble until suddenly they were in an intersection and the river of bodies was splitting in half. "Green to your right. Red and orange up the hill. Green to your right. Red and orange up the hill." Six or seven men and women — respirators dangling off their faces, sleeves sealed with duct tape — stood in the centre of the intersection and divided the ranks. Safety go right. Security say bye. The organizational phone calls between the beer-gutted and the body-pierced were almost audible as shoulders turned from one another.

"I'm not sending my brothers into tear gas."

"Then you're not opposing the FTAA. Seven, eight, even if you have ten thousand union brothers, they're useless if they can't be seen."

"They'll be seen, all right."

"Only by each other. At twenty and Henri de la chase, we can all stand together, fifty, sixty thousand people in front of the fence."

"And when some hothead starts throwing rocks, out comes the gas, the water cannons and the clubs. Then you've got sixty thousand trampling each other. My people have kids."

"Well, great, I hear Nike's hiring."

Chuck had had similar debates with himself. Bewildered at his first pre-protest meeting, bored at the second, he was tested at the third. Find an Affinity Group you can work with. For better or worse, we're going with a traffic-light metaphor. Green's very safe, no danger of arrest, no violence. Yellow will engage in non-violent Direct Action. You might lock down in front of a building or block traffic. Remember, your affinity group will need an Unarrestable. And red, well, you know who you are. Let's get green by the pillar, yellow in the middle, and red to-wards the wall.

Rising slowly, Chuck looked over to the red hot cell. Was this the dynamite crowd? The code kids? Just go, just go. But what if they'd asked him about Mexico or the cabinet ministers he couldn't name? His feet were on the move, but he had no glory from Seattle, no e-mails from distant comrades, so he settled, bilious, into yellow.

Now, climbing a steep wooden staircase, he slid the pig off

his head and passed it up like a concert balloon. He saw someone else shake a stump-leg in greeting, then wave it to the crowd.
Behind him was a stream of bodies, but many of them were backs,
not faces, as family green marched off to the bus park.

"The fence" simply stacked two common construction in-
gredients. A chain-link fence had been set into a string of the
metre-high concrete barriers normally used to divide lanes of
highway traffic. The fence was four metres high by half-a-city
wide. Admission-price democracy rattled in the wind.

Major and minor roads poured together alongside the on-
ramps to two urban expressways. Both halves of the expressway
curved off in the same direction, but one climbed on enormous
concrete stilts while the other tucked low. Plenty of room to
gather, plenty of room to run. Precise rows of black-suited riot
police waited behind the fence.

In high school, Chuck had been forced to study a poem after
some anti-fag legislation was passed. Protesters and police had
both waited outside the legislature as debate became law. AIDS
was the new fear. Newspaper photographs showed the police
wearing latex gloves, white, alien fingers anticipating the blood
they would spill. "Urethane the teeth of your dogs," the poem's
sergeant had ordered. This image returns to Chuck as he stares
through diamond wire over the neat, polished helmets. Big
fingers in latex gloves replayed alongside the phrase *theatre of
war.*

Such a large theatre — ten, eleven lanes of traffic — and so
slow to fill. He dropped his goggles to his neck and returned the
bright blue respirator to a pack strap. See, Dad, it's not so bad.

Amazed to be bored, he strolled about as others poured in.
Everywhere around him protesters of globalization and eco-
cide lit up cigarettes. A man, maybe thirty, wore a cheap devil's
costume and urged everyone to sit down peacefully. Water

bottles were raised and passed. Knees up, shoulders rounded, many could joke with friends and then hurl an insult at the cops with just a turn of the head. Get bored beating your wife? People stepped gingerly around a blind black man who smiled and clapped often. White teeth, white cane and eyes. Wide, pink mouth.

Behind them, the young spring sun grew tired, slipping down over an urban panorama no one was watching. A rare vantage point was carved out by these fat lanes of traffic. The whole city was visible behind them — neat streets and obedient rows of houses that drained into sweeping green fields and the tougher, darker greenbelt of trees beyond. Pacing now in this cider light, Chuck could feel time grow quiet.

Then colour came, a flash of olive green and bright yellow as three tall, skinny protesters — two male, one female, twenty or under, ex-soccer kids all of them — slipped military gas masks onto their faces and pulled a yellow nylon rope from beneath a T-shirt. They ran through the crowd to leap half a fence and sink a hook home. Immediately a trough cleared behind them. Dropping back, the three began to haul and tug on the rope, not needing to call for the others who quickly reached for its tail.

The police had a musical fuse, a faint barked command, a short trombone declaration overwritten by the timpani crash of their shields snapping Roman. *Kwump, kwump* went the bass drum guns, dropping tear gas against the yellow tug. *Kwump. Kwump. Dunk, dunk* — the small, high percussion of hurled rocks bouncing off riot shields. *Kwump. Kwump. Kwump.* Lines of gas, quick and neat. *Kwump, kwump* went the poison cloud on a Saturday afternoon.

Surprisingly, the brain keeps working. That was the first shock. All stations were not abandoned as the hot metal canisters skidded about the pavement rocketing gas. Flee that gauzy cloud. Check left for a billy-club rush. Glancing back from the mouth of a side street, Chuck debated running immediately or stopping to put on his respirator. However brief, this debate cost him dearly.

Once the gas found you, the mucus panic was instantaneous. And the trick was the assault by vapour. Gas, gasoline: liquid. No. Your assailant climbed the air. The white clouds you saw expanding before you must have been just a fraction of the compressed gas. The dense cobwebs hung several metres in front of Chuck, and still every sinus cavity in his face was scour-fucked in a second as an expanding balloon spread back to dissolve epiglottis, tonsils, every accessible millimetre of mouth meat.

Black-dressed protesters ran swiftly amongst the gagging, coughing crowd to snatch and hurl the sputtering canisters back over the fence. When they didn't have canisters, they threw rocks. "Now," someone yelled, enduring a mouthful of gas to rally people back to the inert yellow rope. *Kwump, kwump, kwump.* A man released one hand from the rope to shield his deliquescent eyes but continued to tug, useless and small, with the other.

Chuck slipped down the alley. Looking back from halfway, he saw the first of the weekend's long series of template images. Most of the heads in the large crowd batted left and right as white gas indiscriminately wove between them. A few black-clothed bodies stood firm and sharp, one ninja fist ready to throw. Unique to this recurrent image was the blind man, shrieking and weeping in the front.

Chuck ran back. Light and space flooded each side as he emerged from the quiet alley. A pharmacy fullback, he picked his way through the crowd, racing for the stumbling man. One hand had reached down to shake and release the cyclist's water bottle he wore in a mesh bag off his hip. "Here, here," he yelled, momentarily confusing the man even more until his hand was out, bony and sharp against that plump, panting chest. "This will — this liquid will help your eyes," Chuck yelled, mistaking blindness for deafness but squirting wet relief into each blank, weeping eye. The diluted antacid ran white down the man's dark face, catching on patches of whiskers before dropping down to splatter Chuck's outstretched hand. The man unwound, visibly soothed. "Thank you. Thank-you." And Chuck was on to a skin-head with pink eyes streaming. "I'll help. Let me help your eyes." This time he stepped right in to open the spastic eye with a thumb. His remaining fingers settled into the sharp stubble on the naked skull. Turning another pair of pink eyes white, Chuck suddenly realized he could breathe. His throat was molten and his eyes blinked and dripped, but the credit-card respirator did its job. He turned to the police, breathing, setting his shoulders into their own fence before rushing to another scream. As the minutes turned to tens of minutes and the screaming victims from dozens to hundreds, he began to make out a repeated cry. *Vinegar!* he'd been hearing, as the red-faced offered up four-litre jugs of home remedy.

When night fell completely, the police opened the fence to rush the protesters, driving them down the on-ramps. Two cops marched in formation but wielded neither shield nor nightstick, preferring instead a boom mic and a video camera. One for the clubhouse. Pushing the protesters back — gassing, swinging — they moved their line two hundred metres down the expressway to secure one of the hillside pedestrian staircases.

Most of the protesters had congregated under the over-passes they just lost, and they drummed. Everyone dug up rocks or sticks or car aerials to beat the long metal guardrails or the enormous concrete pillars. Chuck watched a minivan pull up cautiously and was momentarily relieved when two girls and a dad hopped out. The girls grabbed rocks, beat a little rail long enough for a camera smile and dropped the rocks after Dad's flash. Still Chuck kept the rock swinging in his hand. One. Two. Three-and-four. One. Two. Three-and-four. Above, streetlights showed the fog of teargas reach out and drop ever so slowly down the cliff. One. Two. Three-and-four. One. Two. Three-and-four. They were defeated and noisy. They were defeated and allowed to be noisy.

Kermit Is Smut

Auster Rawls is thirty-four years old and high before breakfast on a Tuesday. The 7:15 alarm. The 7:25 joint. Nine o' clock bell. Wednesday. Thursday. Friday. Each morning he slips on his loose, almost-silk bathrobe and passes two vacant rooms before reaching the stairs, empty heat all around him. His shoulder-length sandy hair, untied and pressed thin with sleep, coils around his neck on one side to dangle like a flap. He ties the mess back in a temporary knot while his feet slap their way down warm clean steps.

Sitting in a spacious dining room, Auster cuts and crumbles the grass over his first lawyer's bill. He finishes a tall drink of cool milk before lighting up on another white-cylinder morning. The walls stand patient and unbearable — Santa Fe Sunset, a washed-out orange that freezes each night and thaws all morning, the walls against which he would notice each new tint in Carol's hair. Copper Russet. Blood on the Rocks. It's been eight days since he last saw her. She, too, is thirty-four. She was wearing leather pants.

Waking 'n' baking means dawdling in his robe that much longer. Generally he assumes that his six-year-old students won't recognize the smell of pot. But still, noses everywhere. The grade eight kids. The dog-eat-dog staff room and its fire-hydrant coffee urn. Sweet Mademoiselle Taylor just two doors down, with her smart olive jackets, long gauzy skirts, and a smile that occasionally spills up into the corner of her eyes.

Auster's large open house is pre-warmed by a programmable thermostat. He is divorcing and indulgent with heat. He floats into his clothes, leaping into Mediterranean sail. His shave is becoming impeccable. Neckties weave together in his hands.

"The tie," Carol had said inches from his chest, "the last vestige of male plumage."

"Kiss the pretty peacock."

Those days of tongue before class.

Auster locks the fresh blue door behind him and pockets a small set of keys. The late September sun is noncommittal about both heat and light. Sliding on a pair of large black headphones, Auster waves at Mrs. Charn. She hustles to her Subaru while he blinks the Visine further into his eyes.

The empty house fades behind him, cooling obediently. Davis Street Exemplary Elementary is just five blocks away. Four trips a day, ears covered in music. Auster, you're not listening.

Carol always loved September. Apples and cheddar. Wool again. The last swims.

The Davis Street door shuts behind Auster as he lowers his headphones to his neck. Small voices fill the halls. His blood charges as he steps through the six-year-olds, the healthy ferns. Older, darker heads tug his way when he passes a staff room.

Auster in his classroom kingdom: the back corner desert of the sandbox, the plotting fiefdoms of the reading groups, the magic tapestry chalkboard. Each morning he raises his head and stares out the sly window to the snug houses and tame trees, a fighter before the bell, a skater waiting for the Russian judge, Houdini at the last lock. My moment, Carol.

"Good morning, class." G'morning, Karl.

"Good morning, Mr. Rawls." The daily purr in his ears.

Each skull is so neat. Dunes in the sandbox are tangible to him here across the room. His ponytail swishes back and forth across his collar as his lips make shapes and his lungs spill sound.

"Who would like to start today's reading?"

A sheaf of hands rises, swift and clean.

Class, Auster still hasn't begun, we need to talk about love. Love reminds us life is a gamble we otherwise wouldn't make.

Every day he sees how small their teeth are.

"All right, Jeremy, would you start us off with Mr. Muggs, please?"

And where, pray tell, is Mrs. Muggs? No doubt locked to some whimpering mongrel.

"Mr. Mugzz saw the boll."

More aplomb, Jeremy, please. Reach for the inner truth.

Each child is obviously a reincarnation. Ex-petty statesmen hoard the building blocks. A yesterday booze hag fidgets, furtively eyeing the nearest glue cache. Freud himself giggles in the back corner, chews a pencil. Auster will return every wayward soul to literacy.

"Thank you . . . Jeremy." Was that a gap? Did they notice? It was a gap — now you're gapping. "Who's next?" Hmm, Carol? Squash coach? The entire legal team?

The classroom is heated by two large ceiling vents, heavy grey concentric circles in the discoloured tiles. Bats of heat drop out of them and swarm through little Suzy Derken's angel-blond hair.

"Suzy, give old Muggs a spin."

Auster is a certified Whole Language Specialist.

He knows the Honeywell Lite Touch III better than a thirteen-year-old knows a TV remote. Syncrhonized with every clock in the house. Manual consulted, warranty filed. The features have been sampled: Leave and Return, Autumn Build, Spring Fade. The electronic thermostat faithfully warms and cools the house all day long, prompting his leave and welcoming his return like an omniscient, schematic dog. A border dog.

Hardware store, a simple Saturday morning errand sandwiched between dry cleaner and coffee shop. Children, no children discussed here between the aisles.

"Five years ago, that company was a cardboard box. I've made this thing."

Discounted barbecues forced them to step farther apart.

"Yeah, I was there, remember?"

Their eight-year relationship might be reaching critical mass in front of snow shovels, bags of salt.

"There are other fulfilling options in life."

Sure, sure. Manual landscapes on the Nikon. Reading in French. His five, ten, fifteen extra pounds.

"This the one?" Slim hip cocked, she held up the Honeywell as if Auster were suddenly expected to identify a chef's knife gone missing. Her large day planner bulged in her black shoulder bag. Under the shop fluorescents, he could see why the colouring in her hair was called chunking.

"Auster. Back to game."

"Mmm-hmm."

"This it?"

"Maybe."

"Are you starting something here?"

"You finishing?"

"My customers won't stand by and wait."

She handed him the thermostat and headed for the doors. He usually refuses a plastic bag when shopping, so he was left walking to the Saab he rarely drove with the box in one hand and a receipt in the other. She hadn't paid for a thing all morning, had recently bought new books on self-finance. Staring at himself in the side mirror, he saw OBJECTS MAY BE CLOSER THAN THEY APPEAR printed across his idiot chest.

A programmable thermostat for the mornings, the air warm around them when they awoke. Her Saturday morning breasts under the duvet. Her soft Sunday thighs.

Auster still returns home for lunch, damming the memories one day, loosing them the next. Would he catch her between appointments? What leads would she tell him about over leftover pasta? The crispness of her shirts. The day's décolletage. To suddenly appear in the staff lunchroom would be an admission, a cold, whimpering dog thing to do.

Thankfully music has made life more spherical. Decked out with a new player, a new CD every Saturday, he's learning more than just new songs. The same track list that keeps him occupied throughout the walk to school is just three-quarters finished on his return. Freedy Johnson and Doc Watson know he's racing home. They agree the house looks too solid. Edges sharpened all morning, windows turned to steel.

Shutting the sober wooden door behind him, Auster strides pointedly through the greeting of heat to a tiny auburn box of artificially aged teak. The living-room stereo, also on a timer, throws out some Charlie Parker as Auster sinks into a Swedish easy chair.

Only a few weeks after they moved in, Carol was off to a five-day conference. For a week following her return, she stubbed her toes and fumbled her hands over walls for light switches she had to find all over again. Auster would smile and put both hands on her hips.

The easiest thing would be rolling joints in advance, make a Sunday chore of it. He once thought that taking the time to roll each one would remind him that smoking is a decision, an option. Working his fingers in cylinders and stooping for the lick, he feels vulnerable in the large empty house. Heat isn't magic enough for these ghosts. Parker's demon sax aggravates the tight bramble of shame there at the bottom of his lungs. Carol prefers cash and car to the house. She wants away from everything.

They met through spaces, clinking plastic glasses of sweet but free wine at a Get Acquainted Session in the Education Department lounge. It was the mid-eighties, and they were doing graduate degrees while their friends were making money breathing, taking monthly ski trips and leasing European cars they didn't know how to drive.

"Auster, is it? I'm about to fight my way over to the box of wine. Can I interest you in another glass of Château Hier?

"You already have."

Through a combination of carefully hunted awards and scholarships, Auster could finally afford an apartment to himself. After four undergraduate years of writing essays in the same room where he slept, dressed and occasionally got laid, he now had a desk and a decent reading chair outside of his bedroom. Halfway through September, Carol slid down on him in that one good chair. A caster broke off as she finished. They propped the chair up with books for the rest of the year.

With an unspoken agreement that relieved both of them, the weeks became divided into separate working quarters and several nights over. Carol in a library carrel (him with the recurrent pun), Auster in his chilly, farty apartment. As term picked up, Carol would often work right through to the library's eleven p.m. close before dragging herself the few blocks to Auster's bed. Usually he would walk to meet her, shaving that extra fifteen minutes off his own work but sharpened by the fresh air. Drunk on the fit of her held hand.

"Whole Language, smart title," he started again one night as they neared his building. "It feels like everything I've been waiting for."

"Any better idea of your angle?"

They walked up the stale brown stairway, oblivious to stains, cracks.

"Student journals. Right there on the front lines."

"Get them writing and then start worrying about how they write?"

"Exactly. The animal wants to use language, not listen to instructions. I've been fantasizing —"

"Makes two of us." She reached in for his belly as he slipped a key into the door. "That library."

"Fantasizing about a book. Here, I'll show you."

"Big Boy."

Auster slid the pack off her back and dragged her over to his desk, flipped through an open book. "Look at this." He swung her legs under the table and wrapped around her from behind. "Years of writing with students and I'll compile a whole book of these mind-splitting misspellings."

"Teacher go Zen poem."

He retreated as she glanced over the textbook's excerpts, standing back diagonally to look at her face suspended above the book, a desperate chessboard bishop one move from the jump.

Kermit is smut.	**Yes, Kermit is smart.**
he reds.	**What does he read?**
he eat flyes.	**Do you like to eat flies?**

Carol looked up with questions, but Auster spoke first, hanging on her eyes.

"Buckskin."

"Okay —"

"The brown of your eyes is so soft, like buckskin."

Her sweater came up as easily as a clean shirt off a line.

Supper wasn't their meal. They were breakfast lovers. A kiss-less morning fuck followed by a full pot of coffee. Friday afternoons saw them bursting through his doorway with groceries, Portuguese wine and Carol's knapsack bulging with books, pyjamas, that navy pullover. His dresser creaked in protest as still more underwear exercised squatter's rights. She gave him her favourite shampoo at Thanksgiving. "Call it vested interest."

Perhaps he was rushing things that first Christmas. Regrettably they were both pulling off to strained family relations in other parts of the country. They adopted a date to exchange gifts and started with cheap *mousseux* and orange juice. Carol gave him an obviously too-expensive cardigan and Rilke in hardcover. Placing a small square parcel in her lap, Auster leaned back as she tore off a series of wrappings. One box opened on another. He bit his lip for the vulnerable instant when she finally uncovered the small jeweller's box.

"Oh," she said before opening it, eyes swelling a little. She nervously tucked a wayward lock of unwashed hair behind her ear before prying the lid. Her cheeks split with laughter even before she turned to him. Sitting on the purple velvet designed to hold an engagement ring lay a key with radioactively bright fake gold plating. Smiles in the kisses. They chuckled all morning because he'd been checking. A key masquerading as a ring, teaching small children to read — practising, Carol, practising.

The finish on the key wore off quickly with frequent use, and the cardigan now hangs in Carol's deserted office, the only object in one of Auster's two empty rooms. Rising from the chair's Swedish embrace, he swims to the kitchen, turning up Parker as he passes. Midday sunlight swats at the blue smoke. The answering machine flickers self-importantly in a corner. Just sign the papers, Auster.

Up in the kitchen, the heavens and the clouds, Auster slices a bagel and races alongside a bullet train of half-epiphanies. He isn't cooking anymore, just heating. Breads with cheeses, onion, tomato. Cereal all day long. Sitting in front of the speakers, he nibbles away and thumbs through a student journal.

Naive Cormac Evans:

Suzyz Swing	Suzie's Swing
furst we cut abord	**First you cut the board**
and then the rop	**and then the rope.**
Suzys dad climd the tree	**Suzie's dad climbed the tree**
on a latter.	**on a ladder.**
He teydt four Suziynme	**He was nice to tie it for**
	you and Suzie.

Knots Cormac, watch their knots. He scans the pile of workbooks, looking over the colours and names like pharmacy pills. Julie Phillips for a little sunshine.

Sardonic Peter Loh to take the edge off. Confiding Gabriel Rhodes:

My sistr is stooped and men	**My sister is stupid and mean.**
She taks my thingz	**She always takes my things.**
that she wantz	**She wants.**
I hat her.	**I hate mine too.**

Shutting down, the stereo strangles the saxophone in an instant, and Auster packs up, brushing his teeth on the way out. His headphones are on and giving before the key's in the door.

A few steps and he turns to stare it down. Gould goads him from each archipelago ear. The second-storey windows. Bedroom. Carol's office. Spare Room for Now. He picks up a rock and hurls it. The rock plunks, yes, off the siding. He turns quickly from the glass he purposely missed.

Their friends (his friends?) Jeff and Sarah live in the country. Large house under perpetual renovation. Rattling old Volvo. A hound-shepherd cross named Django runs all twenty acres. Like many dogs, Django did not look the other way when Jeff and Sarah had sex. One weekend when the four of them were together, Jeff described how Django would suddenly leap onto the forbidden bed. He'd bark, or, worse, sniff. When the dog finally started to leave the room or lie quietly in a corner, Jeff would turn his head to call out enthusiastically, Good boy, Django. That night in a creaking old bed, Django became Auster's latest nickname for Carol's crotch. Hello, Django. Does Django want a biscuit? Sit, Django, sit.

Django is not at all welcome in class. Auster tries to stay square in his desk. Mark, mark, prepare. Shoo, erection, shoo.

Without getting up, he slides his jacket on from the chair back and reaches for a file folder. "Keep reading."

Are you afraid of what you want, Auster? She hides in the back of his hand. Her phantom breast still arcs his palm. Tastes are not forgotten. In the staff men's room, the stall walls are a few inches shorter than Auster, so he leans back into the locked door, stringing the bow of his spine with one hand. There are no kids.

Carol, Carol, always Carol. His necktie between her breasts, between her teeth. Drawn between her. Thin, thin toilet paper crumples wet with his quick jizz.

"Jeremy, put the sand down." Do X, not Y. Move the matter here, there. Small authority, he resumes his desk, running out the clock. Coming on two-thirty, the kids are drought cattle for recess. The bells and intercoms are becoming more and more Orwellian. When freedom does come loud and shrill he wades through the hip-high traffic for the pay phone.

The trajectory of university, marriage, job, house had been golden. Hard fought and lucky too. Save by walking to work. Save with a home office. It's not like she couldn't take work, good work, during the pregnancy. Long-term, life-term. Sweet but wrong. Marriage means. Marriage means.

"Jeff, good man, happy afternoon." Auster tucks a calling card back into his wallet. "And how was Oz?" Oz. Oh-zed. Ounce. One ounce of hydroponic pot. Carol has called him simpleminded despite his intelligence. Auster has a friend who smokes and grows dope. Auster gets dumped. Ring. Ring. Auster gets dope. Simple. Minded.

He winds out the day by reading aloud again. (Some day he'll return to teaching addition.) He sets a paint-swatch bookmark aside and feels how his shoulders could jackhammer out the tears.

Open the door to heat. Bird flies from his stereo cage. Now he understands Carol's love of computers, immersive systems and entrenched premises.

It's not as if he's going to smoke away the rest of his life. Just a few bags to get him through the divorce. Might as well be hung for a sheep as a lamb. Just needs to relax. Hates to be alone. Work will get him through. The dope allows him to work and relax at the same time.

Auster cuts Bagel Three with a knife that has rested in Carol's hands, the very point of accusation. He had just returned from a weekend at Jeff and Sarah's. Carol had stayed behind, working. They cleaned on a Sunday night.

"Their kids are really a part of who they are. I think that's exciting." Auster tipped the dustpan into the garbage.

"So long as you find being thirty pounds overweight, stuck in a dead-end job and high half the time exciting." Carol scraped at the stove top with a cloth-wrapped knife.

"Hey, are you all right?"

"Just not interested in excuses."

"Excuses?"

"Forget it. Finish the bathroom?"

"Gleaming."

Auster thought he was walking off until he saw her fading back reflected in the glass of the oven door. When did she acquire this monopoly on exits? He stepped outside.

Like most, Auster didn't look at the stars often enough. Their walks faded out long ago. The sex was becoming perfunctory or combative, and he didn't know which was worse. Sitting on the driveway with his neck against the car's bumper, Auster admitted to his thermostat scheme. If we had nicer sheets, we'd be together more. Silk pyjamas. Warmth in the mornings.

A distant red dot caught his peripheral vision. Two houses down, teenage boys huddled on their parents' deck trying cigarettes. Coughing. Laughing. Just yesterday Jeff told Auster that peripheral vision lets in more light, that's how animals and basketball players survive. Auster wanted to lecture a son playfully on the evils of smoking, tell a daughter about per-iph-eral vision and the stars. Instead he pulled the door shut behind him and clicked the deadbolt. Her work is stressful. Don't be selfish. Buy her a CD. Get that thermostat up and running. We've always loved the fall.

Enough with the nostalgia. He slides a laden bagel under the broiler and makes a quick trip into the living room for a little memory solvent. It's just the roach from lunch. Dinner will taste better. Marijuana Sodium Glutamate. How about a pot of coffee and a crack at Flaubert's *L'Éducation*? Where's the breakfast hitter?

Soon there's much more smoke. Auster gets through the remains of the day and moves on to some quick pipe and lighter work. He doesn't notice the blue wisps rising out of the oven until the second before the smoke detector goes off, just like the dream that unfolds towards the crucial phone call that is actually your blaring alarm clock. Christ, he runs for the oven. Shit, no oven mitts. Throbbing hand, smouldering bagel and wailing smoke detector swarm all over him.

He grabs the nearest fan, a pink student notebook, en route to the smoke detector. Screams of trumpet music rise and fall as the alarm starts and stops. Auster jabs the stereo's power button and storms to open the front door. Smoke and heat stream past.

Staring at the sacrificed bagel, fingers throbbing, he confesses that knowing he's high is becoming as common a realization as knowing he isn't. He needs to get to the source. The Honeywell is only a signpost. His burnt fingers are ambassadors. Just a little more pipe and lighter to bridge the gap. Smoking his way up the stairs, Auster steps into Carol's office. Taking one, no, two, yeah, a final one, he sets the pipe on a windowsill and slides the old cardigan off its hanger.

Descending two flights to the basement, he slips the cardigan on backwards to fully cover his arms and chest like a plutonium worker in wool. Kicking aside the boxes of unused tennis rackets and cracked ski goggles, Auster pulls the chain switch on a bare, dusty light bulb. The furnace, the tall blue heart of the house. He reaches out, wrapping his long, woollen arms around the hot furnace, closing the embrace with cheek against metal. Pain flies in and out of his skin, flapping from hot tin through to bone and back again.

The Body Machine

The umbrella and the bicycle are the two perfect things that we cannot make for ourselves. We know how they work, we follow their operation, they are X-rays of themselves.

— Saul Steinberg

"We'll catch the drop off Regent, jungle the gully, then shoot the stairs at Cumberland."

James doesn't have a mountain bike phrasebook tucked into his bright new jersey, but if these Cool Max kids had said anything to do with stairs — pancake, snort, do the wobble long — the same fear would spike up from his bobbing knees. He has seen slick magazine photos of wiry riders with fatigue overshorts hanging forty-five degrees over wood, brick or concrete. If he had come across a how-to article, would he really feel any more prepared? If a skateboard magazine suddenly ran a detailed article on "How to Suck Your Board Up Horizontally Onto a Long Metal Railing and Drop the Whole Length," better railings everywhere wouldn't exactly be beset by grip-tape ninjas.

Nonetheless, James slips into the pack. Zipping from a bike store parking lot through downtown streets — each stroke one closer to the stairs — they pass several intersections. He could cut away at any moment.

Want a trail? Query a bike shop. Pushers or maybe public servants, good shops host weekly group rides to showcase the local landscape. If a white-bearded hip-breaker rides into the parking lot with a bottle of 7 Up snug in a cage, they'll hit the wide, flat rail-to-trail stuff. For the pimple punks it's an urban ride from staircase to staircase. Lots of spitting and straddling the frame while rude, privileged kids take turns working disc brakes and two sets of shocks to hop laterally up wide steps. Some can make it up and down a picnic table from ground to seat to top and down again. Ask that of a horse or motorbike.

Going urban jungle with this wolf pack of students, the underemployed, twenty-four-year-old James feels conservative and geriatric. He'd come hoping for wooded single track, hardly safe or easy. Having moved here three months ago, he still hasn't found any of the hidden narrow off-road trails that run out of most cities. He wants a roller coaster of orange pine needles and rotting leaves, but sweats his way towards an asphalt lip and a littered gorge behind a strip mall.

Look where you want the bike to go. Ride long and dog, nose to the ground. Use your chest as ballast.

And he flies down, whipped over sun-baked mud, clutching obedient gravity. Lip down, stairs to go.

Callus the pipe in your hands. James is startled to feel the solid curl of the handlebars beneath his fingers. Tugging whole on the pipe, he makes a narrow pass through a ripped fence and throws down more knee for a sharp climb.

Hardback, full suspension, what? Suspensionless? No single word stands shop ready to describe a bike lacking both front and back shocks. At least not one this crowd uses to his face. Antique. Dinosaur. Rec rider. James has tried not to be covetous, but he bought just before shock-absorbing forks and frames became remotely affordable and *de rigueur* on the trails.

With running or cross-country skiing, the vertical thrust of the calves is swept into the throw of the hips. Hunting bigger game, cycling uses the snarling chainwheel to enslave the surly quads. Free of this rotation, one shoved leg would send a body skyward, but the chainwheel seamlessly converts every leap into a roll. Or it did until shocks arrived.

"Load her, Billy, load her."

Before James has a chance to ask for a translation, Billy accelerates on past to leap a guard rail. Leap pedal to haunch. Pedal out of the biped. Others continue the steeplechase, but James slows, stops, and lifts his hard bike over.

"Time for a new machine," a non-Billy says.

Press your own weight down into your shocks to load them with extra spring off a pop. The long flight of wooden stairs running down a steep embankment at Cumberland Elementary could easily show James that he cannot handle the load of his own body.

Vertical reach aside, James holds his own on two wheels. What he lacks in spring he makes up for with smooth, even endurance. Less agile than the feline Billy, more cautious than the loud guy with the enormous head, James pours steady and true, each leg a farmhand soldier. Racing single file through the cloying air behind a Kentucky Fried Chicken, he clocks on ahead and wishes this run poured directly into the stairs, yeah, bring them on.

Until they actually arrive. Swerving from residential street to empty school parking lot, the posse fans out, drunk on width and gunning for speed. Any hope James briefly holds that they cannot possibly be making a run for the grass wall of the hill ahead is dashed by the biker's Morse of shifting gears. Bumping wordlessly over abandoned gravel, they drop chains and let knees fly. They throw it all on the smallest gears, terriers for the rat hill.

Uphill the shocks are irrelevant, and the poor craftsmen stop blaming their tools. A few pounds lighter, a five-thousand-dollar bike is really no more likable to get you up a hill than a five-hundred-dollar bike. Technique is barely relevant. Sit back on the seat to sink weight into the rear tire for maximum traction. Stop callusing the hand pipe. Bet everything on the speed of your spin.

The wide, green embankment takes all comers. Billy and his NASA steed slog away alongside James and the one outcast who dared to come along in cotton. Wick-dry jersey, beefcake T, the hill splits them all the same. Muscles and chains above, along-side and behind. James would never have attempted this hill alone, and yet he holds his own in the slow crush murder for the top.

Avoiding the saw blade of the chain is the primary impulse. Roll back down. Hands out of the fire. Bend the will to snail the razor edge, and eventually you will discover that the dense solid line in your burning thighs is not hill, frame, or even bone, but you, your own strength, muscle returned back to you on a skinny chain. Push ahead of the pull.

Atop the playground hill, sweat drops freely from James's forehead and sheathes every limb. His lungs surge and heave, but the steep grass wall, the entire schoolyard and block after city block spread out triumphantly below. As do the stairs.

The other riders drink and spit, roll about clicking gears and bouncing shocks. Third place in the climb — thank you very much — but now it's downhill. Speed and terribly reliable inertia suddenly seem far worse than the torturous climb of just minutes ago. He could roll uncontested out the back of this rear parking lot. Hey . . . guy, don't leave yet.

He doesn't move. However gruff, spoiled and annoying, these strangers prompted him up a hill he never would have attempted on his own. They can do the wooden chute of steps and rails. They will charge out of the troop-carrying ship, scamper into the cattle truck. The green, weather-resistant lumber quietly leaches arsenic into the schoolyard soil, and James hopes he can see how somebody else handles the drop.

"Okay, who's up?"

A cushion of panic waits at the top stair to take years and confidence off James alone should he approach.

The T-shirt maniac winds back for a clean drive. The frame pulls a new shape out of his plummeting body, arcing the spine past the rear of the seat to dangle ass above the rolling tire. Outstretched arms take the jackhammer blows. A clenched jaw bobs continuously as the rider whips down below them. Tire to tire over stair after stair makes a shockingly steady noise, a hornet monster roar.

James should have gone second with a wordless fuck-it. As is, he waits for the all call, doesn't volunteer, and watches one, then two more work their dual-suspension cable-calf magic. Studying one more angled drop, he sees the finished riders begin to form a spectator's line. The others. If (when?) he goes over the handlebars, all gawky limb and protruding joint, what will protect him from the inertia yahoo behind? He knows accidents command a steady place in the top five killers in Canada, but still he triple-checks his gear and rolls.

King to steward, he hands the job over to the legs and rolls the crank. He circles back for a clean line. While safer in ways than an angled start, this plan gives him some speed before the wooden lip. He can't have generated much, but right now the roll's enough to make him do exactly what he shouldn't. He brakes just as his front tire hits the plangent wood. For an instant, this wild Newtonian grab does nothing but slow him down. Then the front tire leaves Stair One, drops, and bounces, locked, onto Stair Two.

Force never stops. Force transfers, it finds new routes, it has no fixed address. Two, three, four nanoseconds ago, James poured the latent force of his breakfast (composed as it is of distant star atoms and powered by multiple translations of sunlight) into a speed he now denies the front tire. Blocked, force redoubles like a swimmer off the wall to come up his hard front forks, merge with the tail wind of his ass and drive his head forward. The unmistakable sensation that his back tire has left the ground wakes the sleeping king just as the flames reach his chambers.

Having taken with the left hand, so he giveth. Releasing the brakes, James reopens the outlet of the front tire. One relieved breath gets a toe in the door before the teetering rear tire smacks down horse rump. A wild surge squeezes up past riotous guts into heaving chest and dutiful shoulders, while the body-bike unit pounds, pounds, pounds down towards a flat landing.

However brief, a bike is a sequence. The forty-five-degree equilibrium James has so barely achieved is about to meet a flat stretch of plank as the stairs level off into the landing. This patch of flat wood could be a raft magically straddling a tumbling river of stairs above and below. His front tire will meet the flat before the rear and then drop again, perpetuating an endless sibling rivalry and doing what to the flopping body lashed above? To brake is to catapult.

The cold squirts of fear are strongest in the head and shoulders, that advance party of pain. The blind, mule-ass buttocks trudge along. The butt. A last-minute cable from command central arrives from butt to brain just as the front tire goes horizontal. Dropping off the saddle, James levers his own weight back. When the front tire returns to the choppy descent, he eases gut and butt back to the centre and locks in. A cloak of adrenaline falls over his shoulders and back as flat rolls to ragged drop. Fast approaching, the gravel parking lot requires another ass lever.

"Lucky man," Billy says, assuming James will stop to receive this unexpected diploma. But James doesn't want any more spit or small talk, just this radiating, knee-to-shoulder buzz. He nods once and rolls steadily from grass to parking lot to street, private drugs whipping sheet up his body and down.

Each Cut of Us

*Zion is what you think there's no end of when
you have it, then all of a sudden it's gone and
there wasn't really that much of it.*
— Russell Hoban

Paul's driving definitely improves with each divorce. As soon as the hand flashes orange, he's counting cars and checking a blind spot. Cuts through a corner lot before the opposing traffic even gets the green. He monkeybars through third and snaps into fourth. There is no Karla in fourth.

Walking across the hardware store parking lot isn't so easy. I am only this size. I am only from these ankles up. Eighteen hours ago he thought he was happy, in love. Last night, Karla's gift certificate (joint account, he's now sure) finally got him out to the yoga class he'd been putting off for years. At the end of the session, body pegged out on the floor, the breaths suddenly becoming thought one, thought two, he was shocked he'd gone an hour-and-a-half without thinking of or at Karla. What is time in this glowing crucible? The yoga studio doors shut behind him, and everything became dull weight. Shoes, keys, steering wheel. At home he climbed the stairs, desperate to tell Karla about this new flow. She stepped out of the office, her body blocking the computer behind her as he raved about the reach of his crown, about always moving in two directions. We raised and lowered the heart space.

Three hours ago she left her e-mail account open. He was

shattered with a click of the mouse. By the time he's made it into Home Hardware and has found the lock aisle, breaking up has become a game of inches. Does a lie-to-my-face, phone-calls-on-the-porch, sudden-trips-out-of-town affair require a three-quarter-inch deadbolt throw, or should he go for the full one?

Changing lanes, cracking an egg, leaving a relationship — never hesitate. Decide and do.

Christ, this shitting. He shits when he wakes up from a dream of Karla leading a crowded restaurant table in laughter. Loose brown bands fly out of him at 3:17 in the cold morning. He drops again when he wakes up a few hours later, well in advance of his alarm. Mid-morning. After the lunch he can't finish. Before meetings. At the premature end to conference calls he rushes. Foul, ripping work.

On the third morning he wakes up mercilessly sober, thinking first of Karla, not Advil. Downstairs, he unlocks the back door, tugging at the short chain he needn't use. She wanted to be thrown out.

He begins packing her things, this week's script be damned. Afloat on task and tedium (boxes, still more boxes), he lasts a full hour before he smashes anything. They hadn't wasted much time annexing each other's dresser drawers and had quickly found a place together. The requisite deep-Visa trip to Ikea consisted mostly of mutual excitement. Rounding an aisle to thick beech shelves with hidden brackets, they knew they'd found more than a place for books. Late in the spree, when she wanted a hideous pulled-glass vase, he made jokes about frozen Disney barf but rolled the cart towards her nonetheless. Sure. They kissed and he got ass between towering aisles. Now, launching the vase above the driveway, he's not unaware of immaturity, but he's also very pleased with his decision to throw it up and high rather than hard at the garage wall. He likes hang time and the temporary solidity of glass, likes watching the force shift visibly in this arm wrestle of gravity and toss. Smash you, Karla.

She'd laughed, hadn't she, when he called them the gay porn shelves? Thick, naked and strong. Laughs flying out of her like milk from a nose. That look up, gracious and grateful.

Dirk's been phoning steadily. So, sure, Paul thinks, hitting SEND, he'll want to see the latest pages.

```
FADE IN:

INT. DARK LIVING ROOM - NIGHT

Freelance photographer PETER DRAKE and
journalist NICK SYLWARD drink together in front
of an open wood stove.

Steady CU on glowing coals.

SFX: the glowing embers CRACKLE and TINKLE.

A LOG is added from o.s.

SFX: Peter's steady EXHALATIONS fan the flames.

Tight on COALS.

                    NICK
        You said you suspected. Were there signs?
```

```
                        PETER
        Signs. Billboards. A high school cheer:
        "I'm fucking somebody else."

                        NICK
        So you're sure?

    Peter blows on the coals.

                        PETER
        She came home from that course with a
        mixed CD.

                        NICK
        Jesus.

                        PETER
        Started reading her bank statements.
        Tuesday night she'd be excited about getting
        concert tickets with me. The next day she'd
        talk about going away to a Buddhist retreat.
```

When the phone rings, Paul's lower ribs assume it's Dirk, but his entire top — skull, collarbones, spine — cringe as if it's Karla. The nimble, swatting monster of her voice. Two years of you're wonderful, I'm so lucky, thank you. He braces and answers.

"She's a Buddhist?"

"Apparently Get All the Cock You Can is one of the lesser known Noble Truths."

"There's no knowing faith. . . . It took me two years to get over Beth."

"Two years and how much Scotch?"

"You have to live without her, not without happiness. Seriously, what else makes you happy? No, think of something other than her legs."

"This yoga thing. Man, it's unreal."

"Then spend some money. Buy yoga gear. Go more often."

"Class is just once a week."

"Class? I'm sure the big yoga money's in private lessons for Club Alimony."

"I don't know. *I'll be your private dancer, your dancer for money.*"

"Hey, whatever works. And one word about the shitting: cheddar."

Dave and Steve, two of Karla's co-workers Paul has met often enough, stand at the door with a case of beer. Paul knew they were coming — Saturday morning, fine — and glances up at the U-Haul. In the long mirror he can see Karla waiting in the front seat.

"I wouldn't look at her," Steve says. "We're here to help out, sure, but we don't want any hard feelings. Okay?" He shoves the case forward into Paul's arms.

"All feelings are hard." Paul smiles, though. The case is cold, and he sees all the work in a second. Last night's planned errand. The consultation over expensive brands these cold'n'wet guys wouldn't normally touch. Overnight refrigeration. The okay from Karla.

"Thanks, guys. Brekkie?" Paul holds out a bottle.

"No."

"No."

"You go ahead."

"I intend to."

"This work?" Dave reaches for the brace on the screen door.

Karla climbs out of the truck and heads straight for him. He can see her shoulders roll back in that snug New York T. Her tits float punishingly. He wishes he were in his housecoat or a paper yard bag. They have washed, admired, bought or torn off one another's entire wardrobes. Neither could dress without thinking of the other. Scream naked.

"Are you going to move?"

Why doesn't he spit in her face?

The mental e-mails started as soon as he woke up. Mostly to Dirk, though friends he hasn't talked to in weeks suddenly feel like the right audience for "Paul's World Implodes." As the whisky box with her share of kitchen gadgets goes (thank you, Mom, for the Cuisinart; buy toaster), he heads up to the office. As he logs in he notices the K mailbox and drags it to the trash. "Are you sure you want to delete these items?" Absolutely goddamned right. First-date logistics hidden in charm. Suggestive thank-yous. Daring sprays of early lust. Working from home, he once pulled out of a script to e-mail her, the words already whole:

>   we are
>   each of us
>   cut for love

She fled the office and raced to him midday. Cried when she came. Knocked her forehead slowly into his. Live with me. Live with me.

Zinging off notes from the edge, Carol, James, Rich, Mike and, why not, Gary, to say he pissed on the stuffed elephant that came home from her weekend management course only takes so long. Unwilling to step out of the office to the sight of their bed going down the stairs in the arms of two dumb strangers, Paul sinks to increasingly inane web searches. He'd rather not know www.cheatingspouse.com exists. He shuts the door and tries some porn.

"Feel the floor beneath your knees. Open your shoulders by sending the ends of your collarbones out to the walls. Drop, don't pull, your shoulder blades down. That's it. Reach back and slide your calves out of the way to make room for your butt. Make space in your body with each inhalation, then fill it with each exhalation."

Her words unlock his body. Lara breathes forcibly beside him in a small space, coaching his meagre breath. There is no announcement, I will coach your breath, just two parallel spines, four hanging lungs and her bellows nostrils flooding the studio. He wants the rich air she trades with the room. Down to the belly. Fan the ribs. Float the heart. Eyes closed, he can feel the volume of air above him, feel its soft clouds colouring in and out of her left nostril, right, into him, down and everywhere.

Lying back, breathing, he's able to keep his eyes shut while she stands, glad to feel where she is by breath, not sight. "Power the heel up to the ceiling. Keep the leg straight. Pull your knee cap and the tops of your quads down into the hip. Yes. Keep that going. Pull with the back of your pelvis. Stamp a piece of paper with the bone. Okay, take the knee to the shoulder to ease that off. Here, I'll assist."

Eyes closed, knees to chest as he floats in breath, he abandons the clicking tile game of words, sentences. When her strong wide foot sinks into the underside of his thigh, he is burnt with surprise. Already he has learned that the yoga foot is more like a hand, a thing of width, not length. Her foot the complete electrode. She must be able to feel him cheating. Some of the energy that should be going up knee and down floor he spends trying to open his thigh laterally so he can braid his muscle into hers, shake her foot hand, find the body lock.

Funny what comes back. During their weekend on Manitoulin Island — thick socks, long walks, each whole skin suddenly younger, tighter with trust, confidence, admiration — Paul had flipped through a magazine while Karla was in the shower (door left partly open, pink here and there). An article compared the spaces of the e-mail and the paper letter. Sure, a letter can be forwarded or sent to a *poste restante*, but it always travels in a "discrete space paradigm." I have sent this from a late night at a wide table to your morning nook. A popular novel Paul never did finish described a bomb left for someone as "a terrible letter." Although indiscriminate regarding its victim, the bomb, like the letter, nonetheless has an "audience space." An e-mail virus is indiscriminate in both who and where it attacks. The Karla Virus eats all the way back. He can still feel the magazine pages growing damp from the shower of someone he thought he loved. Viruses know both space and time. Eat backwards. *You've changed my life.* Eat ahead. *How can you even ask if I've been with someone else?*

Paul saw the e-mails to Karla, none the other way around, and angle brackets split his skull. Quotation marks would have attacked him with the same economy and clarity but never with the same arrowhead certainty as the e-mail >, Karla's words coming back in her lover's e-mail:

>You wake up sopping or you don't.

She's been gone ten days when her letter arrives in his dirty mailbox. Subtract two for the weekend, probably three in the mail, and this baby's from Day Five in her new swinging-door apartment. The uninvited math clicks away while he heads to the kitchen for matches. The first sulphurous flare makes it easier to believe he's glad she didn't include a return address. When the corner of the unopened envelope finally catches, he has no doubt at all, just flame curling up in his hand. Wherever he is now, he's away from the confusion and rage he'd find inside this envelope. He stands tall and drops the orange bird.

> To: dkiff@shiftcor.com
> Subject: yog again
>
>   She is a cake iced with calm. No, it's internal calm. Volcano calm. I'd give her anything.
>   She had me sitting on my feet again (I just can't remember the names, somethingsan, somethingbottie). No, really, I can do the tuck and sit. She's the same, beside me. Can you do this? Whammo, her head's back to the floor behind her, calves still under ass (what an ass), spine on the floor. No, apparently I couldn't do that. No problem, she gets me some bolsters (official yoga cushions), and I make it part of the way back, lying there beneath her and the ceiling. Honey, anything you wanna drop onto my mouth?
>   How can I ask her out? At class she's swarmed before and after with the tea ladies. But the private lessons, I might as well tuck a twenty into the waistband of her pants. What am I going to do?

Dirk phones within minutes.

"In your Relationship Dictionary, what does it say under *rebound*?"

"Yeah, sure, I know all this, but, man, I'm just floating in her. Do I not act on this? Do I go through the rest of my life thinking of her?"

"The rest of your life?"

"Every time I see her, she rescues my body a little more. No, not just my body."

"You used to see a chiropractor. You didn't pledge eternal love to him."

"He didn't have her brow."

"*Brow*. Oh Christ."

> My plants are dying. Even ivy. My fridge is such
> a fart. I buy garbage, not groceries, time-release
> garbage. (How do single people eat a bag of
> spinach?) I can't finish a bowl of cereal.
> Have stopped cleaning. The toilet is all wool.
> Keep my sandals by the bed. Before Macbeth
> left she'd been complaining about the dirt on the
> mailbox. It's a white mailbox. Clean or dirty, it's
> atrocious. I see that layer of grime every day.
> When she got a book in the mail from Fuckhead
> I made a big deal. A book's not an idle gift. She
> freaked. Just a book. Paranoid. Possessive. Well,
> well. Here I am packing my first book off to yoga
> (G's selected). I'm knee deep in calculation. She
> can read shorts at work. A novel'd have to go home.

You're in trouble when you see them cry. You look beyond the sea of heaving ribs to calm sea ahead, forgetting that the dip and swell will move from her to you. Three weeks before Divorce No. 1, Karen burst into tears when a blow job didn't work out. The hand that dropped him flew to her crumpled face. He was terrified and reaching for the busy ribs. Hey. Hey. When she packed a bag ten days later, he remembered his distance from those afternoon moans, the undeniably private sound leaping out into the still air. Karla was also spontaneously pumping salt near the end. Broke his Portuguese platter and on came the tears. Idiot, he'd been worried for them.

Some chemists think from the equations, seeing past chalk or paper to integration, to warm cohesion. Others use banks of computer monitors and 3D imaging to trip the light fantastic. Paul drives like the old-schoolers who dance their way into reactions, who need to feel how the molecules move and hang. He sees the lane opening before it occurs and is already dialing Dirk by the time he weaves past a cab, behind a truck and free to grey, seventy-four in a residential.

"I'm on my way to yoga, and suddenly I'm terrified I might drop a nut."

"Like a distended test —"

"No, nothing medical. Uh, I'm wearing tights, okay? I'd been wearing some old fatigues, but they're shiny and sloppy. Flop around when I invert."

"Please, tell me more about your new tights."

"The staple move is the dog stretch. Feet and palms flat on the floor, ass in the air. This is my first night for the tights, and, well, you know, ass in the air."

"Are you making sense to you?"

"Panty lines, man, I'm commando. Now that I'm driving, the fruit's feeling a little too close to the air. What if my tights can't take the stretching and rip?"

"Who are you?"

"She walks behind us a lot. Poking ribs. Tapping vertebrae. She's gonna know the south is free. What's the yoga etiquette on this?"

"Give me back my friend."

Paul hears the tires pour into the phone and then himself again. "She chuckles when she comes. How do I forget that? Doesn't giggle, doesn't laugh. Chuckles. Chuckled, I guess. Oh no, wait — chuckles."

En route to a busy strip mall, slipping past a mini-van — Return your movies, breeders — Paul realizes he just triple-checked a lane. This sour note of caution doesn't discourage his full three-lane sweep, but a triple? Down into fourth for the ramp, he wonders if this hesitation is Lara.

Traffic all but stops. Ramp and six-lane road look and feel identical to the parking lots on either side. Three weeks ago he'd have cursed the wait, groaned at the chrome lock, complained when he got home. Now he floats, breathes Lara, smiles to the stereo groove. He's content in line and on his way to buy speaker stands.

His flow snags inside the noisy, overlit store. Is the hamster wheel of consumption really an adequate response to heart-break and evil? He is surrounded by hyperactive displays — Yes, because the cardboard cutout with ripped abs is water-skiing, I should buy a big TV and sit on my ass — and he cannot forget Karla thanking him for being him. Cannot forget *What would I do without you?* and endless wraps in her gracile body. Everything arms, everything legs.

"Can I help you?" A small clerk asks from khaki, denim and indifference.

"Speaker stands."

Minutes later, Paul is about to ask, This is it? Ugly and uglier? when Lara rounds the corner. With. A. Man.

"Paul. Hey, speaker stands. Us too. Oh, Paul, this is my partner Robert. Robert, Paul."

"Hey Paul, what's the damage on those bad boys?"

"A hundred."

"For powder-coated rods? Great."

"Sadly, you don't look like the ally I need to talk Robert out of these."

"Gotta get the sound in your ear."

"See?"

"Think of them as sound bolsters."

"I'd rather not think of them at all."

"Well, I should get going. Nice meeting you."

As Paul drags a box to the check-out he catches Lara's firebelly voice. "You're the architect."

> Subject: NOOOOOOOOOOOO
>
> Fuck. Fuck. Definitely lives with a guy. An
> ARCHITECT. Fucking reclaimed-space open-concept
> air-and-light son of a bitch. What the hell does he
> need speaker stands for? Where's his silence?
> Fuck. Fuck. Fuck.

This time Karla is handing out cards at a registration desk and nodding with her forehead. Men line up and then wait in clusters of two and three, cards tucked into pockets, belts, a hatband (really). They will chase him. She'll open her dress in a second.

It's 4:38 a.m., and he won't be getting back to sleep any time soon. He rolls out of bed and fishes amongst the socks on the floor. Nicola's coming over tomorrow night (is it a date or does she just want to borrow the CDs?), and the toilet needs a haircut.

There's plenty of bleach in the water, so surely he can use the same mop on both toilet and floor. Scrubbing back to white is hardly the soul-crushing job he'd feared. He doesn't dump the bucket into the toilet but carries it down to the porch. Goodbye sooty railings. There's the white mailbox lid again. In the chill morning darkness and his haste, he tucks back inside too quickly to notice the line of pubic hair stuck to the mailbox. Hello Nicola.

He sits in his housecoat at the tiny kitchen table he borrowed from Mark and Suzie. In the cavernous darkness of three a.m. he smokes his first cigarette in eight years. Nicola forgot pack and lighter when she slipped off in a cab. Finding them here on a run for water, he lit up, then sank into the chair with nothing for the ashes. He works in two more thin drags before even glancing across to cupboards, saucers, cups. Now he understands centuries of economic marriages. I, this skillet. You, this axe. He rests his clammy forehead in his hands, cigarette fuming into the still air. The housecoat slides open in both directions. He flicks ashes onto the floor. Fucking filthy anyway.

Driving, eating, the new script — leaner everywhere. Cut to the bone always. He knows rage is the extra push in his jogging, can feel the three-k shift into Fuck you, Fuck you, Fuck you. Sure, get it out with white shoes and a river trail. At what would normally be his halfway point, he spots Karla's haunting ass and caramel hair. Stride long. Pump deep. The barb, the stab of her, can be folded into the run's red toss. Breathe the yoga machine. Glow the orb at each end of your spine. Breathe, breathe, breathe isn't happy or satisfied, knows no wisdom, sees no pattern, just clocks the miles.

So he must choose. Pass her or turn away? Each footfall pulls him closer to the skin he once thought of as his second back. His once-surrogate body chops the air in front of him, gives herself elsewhere. Soon he will hear her small, greedy breath. He will smell her, then be smelled. He cannot forget the loam of her after a run, the old moss ammonia.

Refusing to turn around, he abandons the trail and takes the steep grass hill at an angle. Despite the slash of traffic and the spherical burn in his chest, he settles into this higher sidewalk. Floating the spine stick he remembers an ancient Greek battle summary: We have the height, they the numbers.

> To: phorst@condemned.net
> Subject: Re: saw her today
>
> The hard part isn't living without her, it's living without an explanation. Eventually you'll stop worrying about why it happened and just live with the fact that it did. We get or lose bodies, not explanations.

The second time Nicola comes over she brings a plummy Merlot and a stack of CDs Paul has never heard. Beats couple and stick. Resamples stack then splay. At the door — Where's my belt? I'll signal the cab — he asks to borrow the discs. Calculations run across her forehead before she relents.

One jangly, sugary number plucks him off the couch. Once he's up he slides the couch forward to grab the tubular speaker stands. He makes a triangle of speakers, body, then throws a move. Damn it all if he isn't dancing to this sunny guitar. Half a track is reversed so he can catch all of that slow boil percussion earthquake. He sweeps the spine laterally and tries to flow elbow to elbow, aching so alive.

Enormous Sky White

The lily houses both the female pistil and
the male stamen within a single flower.
Thus capable of fucking itself, the lily is
considered a perfect reproducer.
— *T. Luper,* The Liquid Garden

Grater is Pavlovian over birch. Filthy fatigues drop to mud-caked boots. A pale ass lowers over the wide, smooth, recently felled trunk. Blackflies and mosquitoes descend, burrowing into the stinking nest of his scrotum and swarming each clammy buttock. A few scuttle over his thighs to split the defence. The generous birch does allow him both hands, but one is full of Spanish moss.

Jerking up his fatigues, Grater carefully stuffs the hem of his stained turtleneck into boxers and pants before cinching his belt. The hole he made just four days ago is already useless. Shifting the remainder of his seedlings to the left pouch, he hauls up the bags once more. Many of the experienced planters support their bags with hips alone, leaving the otherwise constricting shoulder straps to dangle at their sides. Grater tries and tries, but the tree-laden bags worm to his ankles in minutes.

His shovel stabs into the earth, and he swings out from the shoulder to split the soil a second before his fingers insert a seedling and a boot kicks the dirt shut again. Fifteen hundred more and he'll sit by an immense fire and bore a new hole in the belt. Denis will peel and suck another clove of garlic to ward off the flies. Alex will sharpen her shovel with a file. Steves will play guitars.

1499. 1498. A jet cuts the enormous sky.

Of course she smokes in Paris. And Courtney can't say, as she would back home, that she started smoking off friends, then just buying in return. She is in the tight sweater of another language and often functions silently. Buys cigarettes with a nod. Someday, surely, she will be able to ask an older woman on *le métro* about the sale at *Printemps* without being thought of as *a canadienne* or an *étrangère*.

Cigarettes are positively prelingual and don't give a damn about your pronunciation. Sometimes they morph into hourglasses. Sand becomes smoke, and time, just occasionally, a friend right there beside you.

Courtney leaves her dormitory wearing sunglasses against the early morning sun. Bottled water sloshes quietly in her new black rubber knapsack. A week ago she bought an orange leather jacket. She has priced cellphones the size of cigarette lighters. Today it's *le musée Picasso*, then lunch with Guillaume. Dressing with the dictionary open, she taught herself adjectives. *Puissant. Féroce.*

A waiter sweeps a sidewalk. Time for a *chocolat*. She'll read. She'll expand her vocabulary. She'll return to class tomorrow.

Three men in long coats seat themselves at a nearby table. Their laughter is loud and frequent. One of them checks a pocket watch. Courtney stubs out her cigarette and reaches for her bag. No, wait. She'll just jot the words she doesn't know in the back of the book and look them up later. She settles back into her seat. The short-haired man in full view gives her a magisterial nod. They laugh again. That fucking dictionary.

"It's spring and she's studying French in Paris, ooh-la-la," muses Alex as she pushes a file around the edge of her shovel blade.

"Yeah, thanks." Grater looks up. The fire is a hub in an infinite wheel of brown nothing. His eyes are still shocked each day, stupefied by the vast Northern Ontario sky and the endlessness of ripped brown waste around him. Todd's hound Sachmo leaps a comb of dead branches, barking at nothing, dirt on his jowls.

Todd and a few others drove themselves here, two nowhere hours west of Thunder Bay, Todd so he could bring the tawny, aloof Sachmo. Aside from the dog, Grater and Alex have the twilight fire to themselves. The crew is either too exhausted or too surly to gather guitars, paperbacks or treasured letters around the constant, six-foot fire that defines the camp as much as the mess tent, cook's trailer or green plastic outhouses.

Alex is a spear-chucker. Two shovel types are available, D-grips and spears. The Ds are more abundant — Grater's lies four feet away, where he threw it after stepping off the field bus. The spears have no horizontal grip at the top, and proponents argue that they save your arm. When you drive a spear into a hidden rock, your hand simply slides down the shaft instead of taking the jar in the wrist. This makes perfect sense to Grater, but he took the D handed to him and tries to ignore the pain that occasionally lights up his forearm before leaping like a spark from his elbow to the base of his spine. Many of the women use spears, periodically sawing a few inches off the top in a bid to work closer to the peasant ground.

The fire smudges one side of Alex's face with a greasy orange light, finding and dropping iridescent dots in her brown, curly hair and dense eyebrows. Even sullied with dirt the eyebrows are strong and confident, aerodynamic ridges designed to cut her through a crowd. Shovel and file fill her streaked hands, and she curves the steel curve. Her elbow drives back and forth, making a slide show of a perfect breast trapped under dirty cotton.

French is creamier in the mouth, cliché, but true. The spill of vowels. The dance of a well-rolled *rrr*. Every *je* is an intriguing whisper. Courtney feels the blade-like severity of English. Anglo-Saxon, she now sees, has always reminded her of *axe*, or *axes*. Except for *cruel*. *Cruel* is a beautiful English word.

Keeping her pocket map beneath the table, she triple-checks the musée Picasso. Le Marais — the rag and skin district. Sliding the map back into her bag, she extracts a cigarette for the walk. Guillaume smokes Gauloises. The dense blue smoke tastes like hay doused in diesel.

The planters are all so filthy. White is supposedly a bug-neutral colour and hopefully a help under the inescapable sun. Second-string T-shirts and cast-off turtlenecks are slowly becoming brown all over, as if roasting in rotten heat. This foundation of filth is built up daily with new stripes of blood, dirt or tobacco spit. The pants are worse, dipped nightly in mud and molested by Jackson Pollack until morning. Army surplus stores across the country have outfitted the planters in varying combinations of pockets, buttons and laces. A used and filthy United Nations drops to the ground each morning.

On the field bus, Grater loves scanning for new combi-nations of sweat and grime. Necks are streaked crimson from scratching fingers. Eyelids are dusted so fine, nostrils and lips edged in powdery grey. In a few more days, the blackflies will be at their peak. Arms, cheeks and necks will be smeared with the repellent but carcinogenic Deet, one more fluid to hold the dust raised by the eternally screefing, kicking boots.

Some nights Grater doesn't bother removing the bands of duct tape from his left hand. His right is ripped free so the nicked fingers can bring him off. Dotted with the crumpled corpses of mosquitoes, the domed tent ceiling has become a projection screen for his nightly desires. Sometimes even Courtney's chin circles with grateful lust.

Stepping out into the museum courtyard, Courtney checks her quaint North American watch, eyes still ghosting with faceted obsession and slices of colour. At least twenty minutes before meeting Guillaume. Her ash-blond hair is tucked up at the back to form a slight cockscomb of her freshly trimmed ends. This pale ridge will guide her through the café, his gaze a confirming weight upon her.

With enough time for a stroll, she starts out across the adorable cobblestones, passing a group of schoolchildren on her way out the gates. Even the children wear interesting shoes. She travels three quaint blocks before realizing she's entering the same *arrondissement* as her *poste restante*. She's now into her third week, and not one word from *Monsieur* David Grates. *Dah-veed.*

The last time she met Guillaume he raved about the '97 Alsace pinot blancs, alternately imploring her to try them at the next available moment and admonishing her for having lived this long in their absence.

I will walk five hundred miles, and I will walk five hundred more.
Crackling music stabs at the tight morning air. Grater stirs
in his cocoon of two sleeping bags, already dreading the ratchet
of his spine. He no longer remembers feeling his toes. The pressure of carrying up to fifty pounds of seedlings for nine or ten
hours a day has squeezed life and kindness from his boots. Steel
shovel. Steel tread. Kick. Carry. Again. Kick. Carry. Again.

"Rise and shine, ya lazy fucks," Potter bellows at the silent,
colourful tents.

Please no frost. Please no frost. Ahh, the usual blue. Zippers
buzz open and shut as Grater evolves from nylon to boots. The
first few steps are the worst. A sadistic cartoon mouse cleaves his
back to replace each vertebra with a whirring circular saw blade.
Every stumble cuts him from the inside out. His swinging arms
lacerate his lungs. The cold bores his nostrils wider before jump-
ing down his throat.

With the sky so huge and nothing man-made on the horizon,
Grater can easily convince himself he is on another planet,
slaving away his final days in an intergalactic work camp. For
most, the working analogy is war. Isolated from civilization.
Bullied and commanded in startling hierarchy, full of hardship
and small wounds, these MTV and microwave children convince
themselves they're at war. Cigarettes go like crazy. Health Science
students light up after two days of bag and shovel. Grandchild-
ren of cancer victims cup their hands around the flame.

Grater squeezes down the bus aisle and falls in beside Alex.
Like most of the vets, Alex has arrived with a pouch of loose
tobacco and decks of rolling papers protected in thick Ziploc
bags. A rectangular cigarette flops and falls in her fingers.

"Tobacco sandwich?" Grater is surprised at this glimpse of
incompetence.

"Been holding out for a southern gentleman."

"*Enchanté*."

Grater pinches the paper into a trough and drizzles in a rash of auburn tobacco. The trick is to frame the hands, hold the back of each perpendicular to the rollie to allow the fingers their maximum length. Packing the fluffy tobacco with the touching tips of his index fingers, Grater presses one side of the paper to the other with both thumbs and begins the slow, steady roll.

"Need a few?"

"More like seventeen."

Across the aisle, Phil writes in a journal and rarely looks up. Four different letters to Courtney sit unfinished in Grater's tent. He mailed three his first Sunday. But now, not hearing from her, filth gathering, each letter turns to bitterness. Courtney, I miss that triangle of skin behind your ear. By the way, I shit beside girls now, and my pockets are full of scraggly moss. The last page he wrote is smeared with blood and mosquito legs.

"Here." Alex turns Grater's legs into the aisle and reaches up to massage his neck. "Least I can do."

Courtney adores the markets. Aligre is overgrown with fresh produce. Wobbly crates burst with cascades of lettuce, tumbles of fruit. Pheasants are stacked neatly beside the grapes. Hares hang from wires. Tiny green berries burst in her mouth. The small black hogs are obscene and thrilling. At Clignancourt and Saint-Pierre she has glimpsed other Parises. African men in robes stroll and call to one another with clicks of the tongue. Huddles of East Indian women pass plastic containers of steaming grains. She has an eye out for something small she can mail to General Delivery, Thunder Bay.

If only she could talk to him. He told her he was lucky, that he'd at least be in a real city every other Sunday. He said he'd call. She tries waiting, but her room is small and crushing. Several germy gashes crack the old brown linoleum, a situation which forces Courtney to the unprecedented extreme of hanging up slip dresses and waffley cardigans. Why have lime shoes if they're not in sight?

Guillaume asked to see her in again last night. She resisted, even when he stepped toward her, pretending not to understand her response. Sometimes his accent suddenly thickens. Occasionally he stares at her lips while she speaks. His are thin, curling easily and often.

Finally Grater is stoned beneath the stars. Before arriving he thought tree planting synonymous with Woodstock. Surely he has read sociological laws in which the presence of dope is directly proportional to the monotony of physical labour. Until now, he's found the nightly fire surrounded by nothing but tobacco and three-chord truths.

A couple of self-styled Marlboro men have dragged an entire tree trunk into the already gigantic fire. It hangs out like the tail of a giant Q. Seated on the ground, Grater leans sideways to rest his elbow against the trunk. His arm squishes another.

"Sorry."

"You're worse than a stranger at the movies," Alex replies from the other side of the trunk.

"Hey Al, you get any?" His head nods after the red dots travelling around the fire. Dirty faces glow temporarily as joints are sucked and passed.

"Hard not to. I knew Frank was holding."

Looking up to track the dope, Grater is delighted to see two joints heading their way from opposite directions. A quick count reveals the spark to his left is one person closer than that to Alex's right. He leans sideways before his neighbour Tony has a chance to offer the grass.

"C'mon, Tony, dig deep. Put that smoke in your lungs and seal 'em up good. That's it. Whoa, now, Tone, just say no to greed."

Grater takes the thick damp joint and settles into the trunk as Alex does the same. Four eyebrows rise in amusement as the short row of lungs draws and holds the dense smoke. They exhale, content and reptilian, before passing to one another. His free hand stops reaching for her joint when her lips simply lower and wrap around his loaded thumb and forefinger. He'd miss the dope if he didn't do the same. The bright dots slowly bounce away.

His tailbone forks. Firelight catches on a moist sliver of Alex's bottom lip as she bums a cigarette. He forces himself to look into the rippling sky and begins to understand that synchronized swimming is an homage to the stars.

She leans away to light the cigarette off someone else's.

"A Dutch fuck," he says as she settles back into their trunk.

"You dissing a Netherlander or making a request?"

"One cigarette off another — a Dutch fuck."

"Most fireside dates tell me about two to a match during the First World War."

"No, no, I was just —"

"Telling me fucking stories?"

She inhales, catching dirt on each cheek and sharpening those unflinching eyebrows in the glow.

"Time for a magnificent piss under the stars." He shuffles off.

Courtney, is Paris really a moveable feast? Myself, I just swallow the bugs that fly into my mouth because it takes too much time to pick them out. I bark snot. Where are my toes? The bug repellent will eat the handle off a Swiss Army knife. By the way, I fucked a hot little number, but don't feel bad, I was *really* stoned.

Courtney is in the small lift of a five-storey apartment building, finally out of a dorm, *métro* station or museum. Guillaume's apartment is part of the real Paris. And it's the best test of her French. As is, her mouth is always full of nouns. The lift, *l'ascenseur. Bouton. Cendrier.* Cubism is the language of migrants.

The lift pauses, a man enters — ox-blood shirt, rumpled black jacket, small yet boxy black glasses. Courtney's knees flex as the lift surges up. He turns and stares her up and down as if it's not only his right but his civic duty. Stern feminist memos pile up in one corner of her mind.

You have arrived, he says in clear Parisian French, dragging a butcher's finger along the front waist of her cords, lingering on the free belt loops. She's wearing her latest find, hemp-coloured cords that fit perfectly across the waist. The button fly is uncovered, and, buttoned and beltless, she's been feeling a little swishy all morning. *The American belt*, he laments, shaking his head.

The French fingers, she replies without hesitation, moving to take his hand from her waist.

Ahh. He smiles, threading his stubby fingers through hers and baring his imperfect teeth. *You joke. Tell me, are the streets still alive? Is every sidewalk still a poem, or have we too become banal?*

Only some of you.

The lift slows to a halt on Guillaume's floor.

You delight my neighbour and kill me.

Then perhaps I should call.

He holds back the door and waits.

What, no pen?

Test me.

48-74-24-47, he intones, dropping each number like a coin into a final machine. His hand withdraws. The metal doors lurch shut. The lift falls away.

Ripping open her bag she hunts for pen and paper, chanting a very English 48-74-24-47, 48-74-24-47. Fuck, fuck. Pen. Okay, paper. Receipt? Ticket stub? Bank slip? All the trouble of a new bag. 48-74-24-47. Paperless girl.

Writing on her palm has been out of the question since an elevator finger met her hips. *Comment, Guillaume? Oh, Kate, une nouvelle amie.* Still chanting, she acknowledges the smear in her pants and scrapes a large red sneaker from one foot. The sock doesn't make it all the way off before 48-74-24-47 is scrawled ticklishly across her sole. Stashing the pen she slides back into the shoe and walks down the hall, squishing *Sorry David* with each convict step.

If Grater's feet weren't magnetically sealed to the ground, if his intestines weren't a party balloon of sabotaging laughter, he might just make it up the hill to his tent.

"Fuck."

Like a hiccup sufferer, Grater is shocked into silence.

Alex storms down from her tent, head shaking.

"What's the story?"

"Charming Frank has decided to lie in wait *chez moi.*"

"Want a large rock and me to say something?"

"No. I'll get him out, but fuck if I want the fight."

"No problem. I've got two sleeping bags. You get the couch, though."

At his tent, Grater stoops and fumbles with the zipper. "Just give me a second to pull one bag out of the other." He dives for the hardened pair of boxers he's been wiping himself with each night and stashes them beneath a knapsack. He volleys a few clothes deeper into the corners before separating the bags. Poking his head back out, he sets his boots beneath the fly and opens the door wider.

"Come on in. I decorated myself."

"Spare but elegant." She leans back for her boots. The zipper seals away the last sparkles of camp light.

Grater starts with his multiple pairs of socks, shoves a jacket and a few of today's shirts alongside him. He rolls onto an elbow just as she raises her hips to undo her pants.

"Well, nighties," she says.

"Right."

He's about to invite her to elbow him in the ribs should he snore when all hope is lost. Zzzzeeeeggghhh. Mosquitoes in the tent. Both heads flinch and shake. Their ears fill with terrible wings and each other's defensive snorts.

"More than one." Alex sounds every bit Tango Charlie. She frees an arm and starts swatting. "We got plenty."

"Let's take 'em," Grater all but bellows, zipping out and rising. He rests a flashlight in a mesh ceiling pocket, dappling the interior in military strobe. They're both on their knees. Alex guns a wall, shaking a mosquito loose before catching it with a quick clap.

Grater pounds up his thigh. "You be Luke, I be Han?"

"Keep hoping."

Their teeth occasionally flash in anticipation. Mosquito corpses soil the walls and fall from sight.

"Your ass, your ass!"

Not wasting time with detail, Alex catches both cheeks, one after the other with a slight twitch of the hips. Her palms come up victorious in the gauzy light.

"Remind me never to meet you at high noon." He chases a renegade into the ceiling.

They turn towards one another, scanning the distorted light. Scabs, dirt and dead bugs dot their hands. She knows his stomach is flat and hard with work. He's just inches from filthy, filthy pussy.

They dive. Stained cotton scrunches into quick handfuls. Lips make mutual shapes. Tongues go feral. One of them may be eaten alive. She sinks to her back, pulling away long enough to nod at the suspended flashlight. "Nix the floorshow."

Lowering back down, he rifles up her shirt, scouring the slow fabric of her stomach with whiskers, lips, teeth, then tongue. Sucking up a thigh, he's surprised to find absolutely no fat. No dangle, no slack, just inch after inch of solid, lip-bruising muscle. Her panties are down in two jerks, releasing a small wind of copper and cream. Fingers are manic in his hair. Nails scratch fruitfully over his unclean scalp. He sucks and licks from hip to hip as if sealing a secret envelope. Grazing, he flattens his tongue and lays it to one side for an exploratory lick of the hide. Even he can feel her fingernails loading up with grime.

Wrapping her arms around his neck, Alex rolls Grater onto his back, bulging the tent wall to land on top of him. Descending, her hair brushes up and down his damp, hairy thighs before she seals her lips around a testicle, sucking it away from him, then rolling it back, hunting it up his body and down. Her fingers take each testicle with a jeweller's care, pulling them apart before working the seam of his scrotum with just the tip of her tongue, squirming him woman. The neat hole at his tip blubbers with early pleasure.

"So what happens now?" she asks, a hand around him.

"I've got condoms."

Unfortunately, Guillaume goes on about the late morning sun. Fucking him is no problem. Her clit blossoming in his mouth again and again is a genuinely nuclear pleasure. But he insists on the full mean light of the window. Any other time, with any other foot, Courtney would be *en accord*.

He bites down the inside of one luscious thigh, sucking it slowly like St. André cheese. She keeps her left foot flat on the sheets, praying the ink doesn't run. Oh Christ, he's being egalitarian with the legs and has switched from right thigh to left calf, driving his tongue into the knee cleft, raising the leg and massaging the hanging muscle. She tries wrapping the leg around his slick back. Regrettably he takes this as an invitation to grab her by ankle and knee and munch calf as if it's barbecued. A greasy thumb strokes the inside of her ankle. Fingers knead her fugitive foot. Her crotch is now molten, and he's looking every bit like a toe man.

Thankfully Courtney has read her share of flaky Tantric sex guides. A med-school dropout who spent six VW weeks in India back in the seventies whispers in her ear, reminding her that a woman tosses her head in the direction she wants a lover to serve her yoni. Flood-victim Courtney nearly throws a seizure to bait her man. Fuck it. She grabs him by both nipples and pulls him into the lunch.

Grater peers into Paterson Travel, shifting his aching feet on the sidewalk. The crew is generally bussed into town after Saturday's plant. They invade a hotel that doesn't mind admitting ten to a room, wash torrents of dirt off their bodies, then hit a bar. With most stores closed on Sundays, planters traipse between laundromats, tobacco shops and all-day breakfast specials. Twice today Grater has started into the closed post office. Paterson Travel is similarly dark and frozen. Checking the locked door for the fourth time, Grater doesn't notice a shadow slide across the display window.

"A boy can dream, eh?" Alex glances from the window up to his face.

"The pancake-eating contest lose its charm?"

"Something like that. You didn't get far."

"No, but I'm thinking about it."

"Eight hundred to Paris. Gotta put a few more in the ground."

"Really? Hadn't thought of that."

"What about Iceland? One night on the rock will get you cheaply to gay Paree." She nods at Air Iceland's list of two-for-one fares.

"I'm a little short on the *two* part, and a home cloning kit would never clear Customs."

"*Un, deux.*" Alex points from his chest to hers.

"Isn't that a little awkward?"

"I'm a big girl. And you?"

"Still a wee one."

"Flat chested and downy?" She digs a hand into his tight stomach.

Grater is twenty-one years old. He doesn't clarify that she wants to fuck him for the next two weeks and then accompany

129

him across the Atlantic in pursuit of his girlfriend. He glances up the street. Two kids light cigarettes. Another beggar sleeps on the sidewalk. Hooking a thumb into the top of her jeans, he pulls her face into his to whisper *hôtel* with a silent h. The box of condoms in his pocket taps against his thigh as they walk.

Later, they descend into the lobby with growling stomachs and larger hair.

"Bus is fucked," Todd grunts, the proprietor of bad news.

"What?" Grater demands as post office doors open inside his head.

"Alternator. We're here until tomorrow morning."

"Pizza? Chinese?" Alex asks. "Seafood?"

Their Thunder Bay is only a few blocks long. The beer store. A bar with live music. Heading back to the Shoreliner Hotel, tipsy on slick red wine, Grater sees they will pass the travel agent in minutes, and there's no excuse for another route.

"Well," she asks, "you in?"

"This is a bit sudden."

"So's life. If we don't buy the ticket first thing tomorrow, when do we?"

"Know anything about their cancellation policy?"

Standing on a hilltop, shoulders aching with the weight of his bags, Grater can see the horizon dip and bend with the curvature of the planet. The whole vast sky seems sucked down and bent around the scarred, barren earth. He finally understands that gravity isn't necessarily a downward pull. Gravity is the tug-of-war of mass. Moon-bound rockets spend three-quarters of their fuel fighting the pull of the earth and the final quarter resisting the pull of the moon. A fork falls to the floor because mass gathers.

The fucking is better as the dirt accumulates. Filthy, ass-spanking fun. He may have swallowed a bug off her teeth. There have been tremors as he finished her with duct tape covered fingers. Undoubtedly they're licking Deet. In the middle of another beast with two backs, Alex utters today's three magic words.

"Come inside me."

Grater breaks stride.

"I'm on the pill. Come inside me."

He withdraws and reaches for the slick condom. She swats his hand away, then reaches into a pocket of his knapsack. His knife clicks open. He can't have unprotected sex and not tell Courtney. Alex saws off the condom's tip and rolls the remainder down into an impromptu cock ring. She guides him back in with a perfect little sigh. Her hands fix into those two small pools at the base of his back, driving him.

Walls Thick Enough

Now Lorna wants Express on Friday nights. Sure, she's bound to see a few other students pass through the Superstore, but bagging condoms just cracks her up — bag, bag, bag.

The opening of the Superstore last October was the closest the white-collar, white bread city of Fredericton will ever come to a military coup. Gobbling up a sprawling corner lot, the Super crowned itself emperor with its in-store pharmacy, photo-lab and postal counter (what Lorna sometimes calls the three Ps in a pod). All of this and canned tomatoes twenty-four hours a day. Late night Rolo ice cream. Half a cake after midnight. Desires sated twenty-four-seven, Fredericton is aflutter.

Residence is a necessary evil. Sad but true, this was Lorna's mantra. From her hopeful days of rural high school to her mid-afternoon arrival in front of the brick shoebox that would be her home, this was Lorna, young and already rationalizing. Sprung from her hometown, yet soon to be chained in debt, Lorna stepped forward into her cube in the box. The stale, vacant room seemed more excavated than constructed, as if no one living today could be responsible for this uniformity. Surely these pea-green walls were not built but uncovered, geological peculiarities disinterred with chisel and mallet. That compact bookshelf must have been a consequence of ancient seismological forces. A bygone austerity produced that lonely bed.

She's always been chubby, always. Fat girl, she would be pitied and sneered at here as at home. The world would never stop noticing the breadth of her beam. Dropped eyes. The assumption she's pleasant, sympathetic. These were problem enough, and now living in residence means the other side, too. Slim Ashleys bring home trippy young men with sculpted facial hair and retro clothes. Incense and pot smoke precede giggles then moans. Guitars arrive. She wrote *ladder* in thick black marker inside one of the drawers of "her" new desk. Down the hall, someone restarted the Hip's "Courage."

Twenty-four hours. The whole town feels let loose and urbane. Hosts run for cornstarch or custard at the last minute. Rapacious lovers score post-coital pasta. Drunks head for the mouthwash at all hours.

Merchant or maybe warrior, Lorna can't say exactly why the gossip's important, just knows to keep sharp. Other students can scarcely remember their professors' names, while Lorna pieces together the entire faculty fiefdom like a detective casing organized crime. Departmental rivalries are easily discernible in the produce section. Dean Clark takes an obviously sharp turn at the grapefruit wagon to avoid Dr. Baley. Competing biologists steel their eyes across display islands while hefting melons and cantaloupes in a flagrant arms race of fruit. There, aisle four, an affair is brewing. A woman in a long, strident overcoat lingers among the baking supplies as a jacket-and-casual-pants man skims by the puddings and Jell-O, beelining to her scent. They feign a cart crash. He smiles often, retriever-like, while she drops her chin with a more playful, *excusez-moi* flair. Blocked as they are, she asks him to reach for that high-shelf condensed milk. His jacket rises up his mustard shirt with the stretch, and Lorna can feel this career girl give his ass the once-over. Condensed milk, right.

Lorna reaches for her phone, never losing sight of her subjects and swiping can after can all the while. "Dee, pair at the top of four. She just had him reaching for condensed milk. I've got a loonie saying the milk winds up reshelved in five or six."

Seconds later, Lorna looks smugly over at Dee as Reaching Milk Man begins pointing into the cart of Ms. Overcoat. Overcoat laughs as Milk Man points and jokes his way through her week. Dee doesn't need to look back to Lorna to see her gloating. Each of them knows Milk Man is bra-strapping.

"Canadian reserve is like our cheddar, white and well-aged," Dee has heard Lorna preaching over expired iced tea in the cramped staff room. "Witness the grocery cart. Two acquaintances bump into each other. Hi. Hi. Been ages, love. We've all seen near nervous breakdowns and boiling infidelities in the aisles, but how often do we see someone simply gawking into another's overflowing cart? No, no, wouldn't want to acknowledge that we can actually see the bum wad and the large Nutella. Step over to the laundromat and we pretend we don't see each other's goodie gear a-spinning. Flirting, really desperate flirting, is the only time they bob their heads at the carts. Num-num this and oh you're filthy that — it's the only reach going." For a second or two, her monologue hung in the staff room's stale air.

"I want a new one," a customer now demands of Lorna, shoving over a can of Whiskas. "This one's dented." Wading through a rush, Dee and Lorna finally return to the contested can of milk. Lorna summons a pimple-stick stock-boy and instructs him to comb aisles five and six for the milk, making it sound like a lost family heirloom.

A young woman with an actual sunflower in her hair arrives with a wicker handbasket filled with broccoli. Lorna's hands begin sweeping green from scale to bag without the slightest tremor. Politely announcing a total, Lorna hopes this flake from her Thursday religion class doesn't recognize her walrus hips trapped here in a polyester uniform.

The stock-boy stops at the end of the line to shake his head and spread his empty hands. A suited man with a cool blue shirt arrives before Lorna's response can even taxi onto the runway of Air Nasty. Her eyes work up more and more of the customer as she tallies. High-end frozen entrées. Crisp suit. All-natural ice cream. Trim beard. Tapenade. Tzatziki. Pink lips stranded beneath his whiskers.

"What a fine tie," she observes post-pesto.

"I wish I could say the same." He points an eyebrow at her thin and obligatory cravat covered with store-brand cookies and trademark symbols.

"Not a fan of the Lemon Nests?"

"Too subtle."

He smiles and reaches to bag his own. Neither of them notice the increasing fastidiousness of Lorna's grip, the precision of her fingers encircling every can, cornering every bag. For the first time, Lorna gathers groceries from her triceps, weighing every morsel. She reaches for Mr. Cool Blue Shirt's last can and then looks up, caught.

"Richard Peltor," he says slowly as Lorna encircles a lone can of condensed milk. He lays out a line of crisp twenties and walks off with his already bagged groceries, leaving Lorna heavily tipped and speechless with cream.

"There's no price on this." A man shoves a slick tray of chicken wings into Lorna's limp hands. Before leaving that night she schedules the same shift next week. In Fredericton, only lawyers wear suits.

Richard flirts with Lorna tirelessly. His jokes are nimble but modest — one laugh per. Her shirt buttons pop open, pop. (His hand scoops at his body.) He will feed her chocolates, then last forever. He sits on the edge of his bed, stroking, his posture a crescent of restraint. Lips snarl into jaw clenched. Lorna with a cool wet jewel for his forehead. The tail of his spine wags inside his pelvis with the flashbulb orgasm.

Lorna stops by the Superstore even when not working. Low on stamps. The dorm soap smells and feels like pig fat and sawdust. Toothpaste. The twenty-minute walk from campus is meditative and relieving. One more day to the one-week anniversary of condensed milk.

Sure, she could wash her uniforms in the residence laundromat or even one of the two commercial venues between her dorm and the Superstore, but the Super's dry cleaner is into trade. As in prison, the cashiers are divided into temps and lifers. Each lifer deals in her own way, but mostly they smoke. They smoke, or want to, far more than break time allows. A mobster with an iron bladder, Lorna often works through her break to let a smoker go in her place.

The electric doors sweep aside to reveal a dour Fran at the dry-cleaning counter.

"Hey Fran. Need a break?"

"No, Lorna girl, but thanks. You on tonight?"

"Just here to pick up a few things and" — Lorna rolls a shoulder to emphasize the weight of her laundry-laden knapsack.

"Christ girl, give it over."

Lorna unpacks a couple of skirts and some uniforms.

"Keep this up and I'm likely to get your skivvies next."

Strolling the floor out of uniform, Lorna undercover. Is it the height of the ceilings that gives the lonely those little Please Chat halos? "Hmm," Lorna mutters over a pyramid of lemons. She doesn't look directly at the elderly woman beside her, just tosses her chin. "Not very nice, are they?"

"Watch the skins, sweetheart. Stay away from anything too thick or porous."

Lorna would like to plant a radar gun in aisle two to confirm her theory that people travel faster past the toiletries and cleansers. At checkout, even the most talkative customers clam up at the wad and liners. A few even rise to bristling condescension.

Rounding a corner, she sees Richard scrutinizing the side of a can. Backstep. Hold. Breathe. Fran.

"Fran," Lorna gasps, shutting the rear door of the dry-cleaning kiosk behind her. "I need my uniform back. Quick." Lorna begins rifling through the bagged garments without acknowledgement or approval.

"Easy, girl, leave a little on the hangers."

"Fran, help."

Assiduous and perturbed, Fran slides her archivist's fingers through the rectangular sheets of cloth. Lorna peers out a blind-sliced window.

"He's coming."

"Not without you, I hope."

Lorna grabs the shirt and dives behind the long coats and blankets. Still tucking her shirt into her very non-uniform jeans, she reaches for the phone. "Mary. Lorna. Blood feeling a little low? How 'bout I tag in for a few minutes?"

Sliding to the helm of aisle three, Lorna squeezes a loaf of Wonder and sees Richard. Yes, he's looking for a checkout, but no, he doesn't — crash, a pickle jar drops from her hands. So sorry, so sorry. Her gulping, guilty look breaks when her eyes meet Richard's.

Unconcerned where he stands in the fresh brine, Richard passes over his OJ.

"If indeed we are what we eat, you get to see a lot of people."

"Too much of most, not enough of some."

"You're certainly seeing me. Would you like to share some food that doesn't come out of a box? Maybe Zal's this Friday?"

"That would be lovely."

To Take a Man on a Hill

Edward Sprat first read Donne's line "No man is an island" with rich dark hair and a shit-hot mile. April 1997, however, finds him all let out. A full gut drapes from his jawbones on down. The thatch of thick hair is long departed. He pushes glasses up a heavy pink nose and pulls *The Globe* closer to his ruddy face. PEI Bridge Up and Running.

Prince Edward Island is to be finished off on foot. The thirteen-kilometre raised concrete chute of the Confederation Bridge will officially open with the heaving limbs and collective sweat of a race. Linked forever to the New Brunswick mainland, Prince Edward is no longer an island. In just thirty days, runners will swarm the body of the giant. Jason's got the hunger, but Kyle's got two years of muscle on him. Tough call.

Rising for a second Scotch on company time, Ed pictures ocean sparkling on each side of him and the whip-snap of those two tireless motors he once had beneath his buttocks. Every few weeks he likes to slip out of the office early and enjoy a few hours to himself in the house. He doesn't find much. No vibrators he doesn't know about lurk in Cheryll's drawers. The boys still aren't hiding dime bags of pot. A few condoms, some girlies. Years ago he found his track scrapbook under Jason's bed.

The sound of the garage door opening is not followed by the roar of Cheryll's wagon, so Ed doesn't bother to knock an inch off the top of his Scotch.

"How many of you?" he yells as the side door creaks open.

"Two and growing."

Thuds fill the hall as laden knapsacks and behemoth sneakers drop to the floor. Two blind rooms away, Ed can feel the fringe of blond hair that swats about Jason's eyes as he leans forward to work off the heel of one shoe with the toe of another. Kyle raises one foot behind him, then the other, to slip off the heels of his sandals. "You eat?"

"Zoning," Jason replies.

"You both going?"

"Yeah, I'll grind him," says Kyle.

Two glasses hit the counter and the Brita gives it up clean. Four large feet thump up the stairs. Today's skirmish over socks doesn't last long. Tumbling back down, the boys head to the TV to stretch with videos blaring in the corner. *Fat girl ticklish.*

Kyle and Jason pull themselves into the run. Four legs reach and release. Two spines emerge from the caves of their days.

"See her again today?"

"She's in my bio class. I see her every day."

The mere twenty months between them has always translated into two full years of school. Now, at fourteen and sixteen, this difference is the castle wall between middle and high schools. Junior Jason.

Kyle rolls his neck as he exhales. Generally they chat only while warming up. Each of them knows the wisdom of starting off slowly. Feed the ungulate thighs. Running too quickly too soon jeopardizes the entire run. That's the simplicity of running —

pain and pleasure teach patience. But wisdom can feel sluggish. Who wants to be the slow man? Today it's Kyle champing at the bit.

The feet dig up oxygen in the reach for that corner where the ache becomes the energy. Hearts, lungs and legs search out that wrestler's moment when you can pin pain itself. Elbows occasionally glimpse prior life as fins. Each head wears a plume of steam. Running uphill curves you backwards until your hands practically slap the base of your back. Your only hope now is to dig beneath your ribs and rip your stomach out whole. Toss the sphere of guts by one long intestine to bob over your shoulder with every stroke. Give it one inch too many and the dwarfing, downhill contraction will toss you into your own somersault.

The tumbler is rinsed and already in the dishwasher, so Ed doesn't get up as Cheryll pulls in.

"Well, sweet thing, how was it?"

"Hey," she replies from a whirlwind of bags, keys and overcoat. The keys half make it into a bowl, the coat slides off the chair it only barely reaches, and her bags fall over each other like blind kittens. Each of these losses to gravity would be increasingly irksome if she stuck around long enough to see them. Bolting for a slashing piss, Cheryll emerges from the bathroom to step calmly over the fallen bags and rumpled coat.

"Small stuff, small stuff." She heaves three-quarters of herself lengthwise onto the couch.

"Yes, they're both out." Ed rolls himself over the creaking arm of his easy chair to land on all fours. They still talk as if they're the dick-in-hand young couple of fifteen years ago. In fact they talk more, outdoing those hiked-skirt bathroom feasters who let wine run down tight chins to naked chests, who crept over sleeping boys, who installed a lock on the bedroom door. Talk is through the roof. Action, there's the nose dive. Here he comes crawling slowly across the carpet. He'll butt his head against one hip and bite his way up a thigh to sniff and snarl over her Dry Clean Only clothes. He'll ask, "Where's your sweet crotch?" but all the while butt her arse farther into the couch, shoving her into the very doze that will incapacitate those once-jerking hands and eager legs. By now he's lost one eye entirely to the pillow of a breast, and his head, filthy lips and all, isn't going anywhere, at least not until one of them gets cramped, crowded or thirsty.

So much shoving in the house. Kyle and Jason crash back into place. Whip open the fridge. Slam down the glasses. Chug it all back.

"Well?" Cheryll asks, trying ever so patiently to bring language to the gorillas.

"Twenty-nine thirty-eight," Kyle pants in reply.

"Not bad, boys," Ed chimes in, elbowing his way through to the fridge. Ed's been showing his beer for as long as the boys can remember. He rarely refers to his girth as anything less than prestigious. "Just more of me to spread around." More money, more charity, two more educations. (More pollution, more consumption, more Ballantines.) In his teens, though, Ed cut grace whole from the air.

The boys were glad when Ed moved the biscuit tin of old photographs and medals to a lower shelf in his den so they could reach it without having to ask. They never tired of teasing him about his boxy crew cut but nonetheless raced to the hall mirror to prop up the new potatoes of their biceps and holler back to ask how old he was when his arms, legs, shoulders were this big? There had still been trophies out when they were young. Even now, old Hills Bros. coffee cans sit crammed with medals at the back of a basement cupboard. Ed set records at the scholastic, municipal and regional levels. He ran the provincial mile every year for four years, always placing, never winning.

Ed planned only slightly, usually just opening the doors he found in front of him.

"How far's a mile, Dad?"

"When you walk home from school, that's about a mile."

"How many miles is it from school to soccer?"

"Probably five."

"How do you know?"

"You get used to it. When I was young, older than you are now, we'd practise at least five miles a day at track." Really only Eddy and two or three others practised every day.

By the ages of eleven and nine, Kyle and Jason were already racing competitively. If he were there, which he almost always was, Ed would linger on after the boy's races to watch the older kids run the mile. On the rare occasions when he did miss a race, Ed would wait until the three of them drove to school the next day to ask about "some of the winning mile times." One night while getting tucked in, Jason asked about Ed's best time. By the next morning Kyle was already complaining that Jason got to hear first. The Sprat Mile of '72 became legend with just one or two tellings.

4:32.6. At eighteen, Eddy chased angels. Second in the province. He loved the mile because it reached past strength to dip into endurance. But he could always see the end. He was personally invited to join several university teams yet left his cleats in his boyhood closet, knowing he'd never make the Olympics. One mile in four-and-a-half minutes, and Ed within them.

Always this circle of hungry men. Amazed, Cheryll watches as the nightly assembly line of arms endlessly drives fork and knife or shovel spoon. At least Ed clears his mouth to speak.

"Hear about the bridge race?"

"Where?" The boys reply in near unison.

"I said *bridge*."

"Mactaquac?" Kyle asks uncertainly.

"PEI?" Jason demands.

"Thirteen and a half k. End of the month."

"How'd you find out?"

"How do we register?"

"There isn't a minimum age requirement, is there?"

Older, Kyle has always been faster. To the stop sign. Around the block. False start. Quickly enough, they were training. By ages twelve and ten they were running three times a week.

"Ky, I'll be faster next time."

"You'll never be faster."

Cheryll was alarmed at Ed's reluctance to make peace. Certainly Kyle should slow down to train with his brother. She slid those ribs, chambered each of those hearts. This glimpse of parental disagreement was all Kyle needed to keep the edge up. Finally Jason himself broke the deadlock. If he was too slow to accompany his brother three days a week, he'd train six. And he did. Still Kyle had the advantage. "Keep trying," he might taunt from the computer as Jason laced up. "How slow?" he'd ask on Jason's return.

Kyle slips through the door, kicking shoes into the closet, tossing a knapsack into a mute corner. Dropping onto the couch, he reaches for the remote. When Much goes to commercial he cranes his neck to peer into the laundry room, confirming Jason's absence with a glance for singlet and shorts. Just a week to PEI. He'll get back out tomorrow.

Shuffling up to the fridge to drink milk from the pitcher, Kyle can easily picture Jason here doing the same or reaching for water after a run. Jason sheathed in sweat. He'll stare out the window at the big swaying maple out back, one hand driving a large wet glass to his mouth again and again. Adrift on his braided forearm, Jason's watch is already reset to a bank of zeroes. Rolling up a belch of cookies and milk, Kyle moves from Jason's blank watch to his lips, suddenly mumbling if asked about his time. As kids, it had been Jason who put an end to discussions of Ed's mile. Ancient history.

Bursting from the house in an explosion of flopping sneakers, flapping laces and loose jersey, Kyle alternately thinks bending to tie his shoes will be stretch enough and that this is crazy, Jason's just running. The unprepared muscles are hard shafts beneath him. The metronome of his brother's legs beats somewhere in the near distance. Jason races pain itself. Block after block fall to his legs. The shoes strike light and clean. Kyle cannot clear mind, legs or lungs. Loops of piano wire wrap his palms to cross-cut his stomach with every stroke. Jason has not been running with Kyle to make himself faster. Jason runs together to slow Kyle down. Kyle takes the reverse of their usual route, the slow lion in the pride.

4:32.6. Eddy's mile, Jason's mantra. No longer numbers, just sounds. Four. Thirty-two. Six. Five beats. For years Jason longed for a four-beat time. 4:32 would have been a cake tempo. Hundreds of kilometres were necessary to unlock the power of that fifth beat. He doesn't count, doesn't intone, just swats, tags the sound with breath.

Kyle looks for his brother to emerge from the distance like the image in a developing photograph. Chew the cramp through. A winged dot grows in the distance. A low-flying bird races up the other side of the street, Jason striding over the pavement. Kyle crosses to meet him.

Surprised, each of them realizes he has never seen the other run so clearly as in this collision course. The running body is halved, left channel, right. Shoes just flick, flick. Navels are about to collide.

Jason smiles. "Wrong way."

"Don't." Kyle puts up a hand, thinking it enough, and is startled at the arc of Jason's hips as he makes to dodge. Kyle has to speak again for Jason to twist out of gear and turn back towards him. Reaching for Jason's watch, Kyle is too intent on checking the line of revealing numbers to see the hand shove into his chest.

Energy crackles up their ready legs, fluid arms and set jaws. Jason's hands are raised. Kyle hopes his breathing doesn't sound as laboured as it is. These fists and noses haven't met for years. Every limb is ready.

Jason restarts from the hips, uncoiling from heel to head. Kyle watches the yellow bottoms of his brother's sneakers recede into the neighbourhood, the underbellies of two fish swimming higher and higher above his head. Jason turns at the next stop sign, taking the Lockmore hill for the way home. Kyle is cement, his run barbed wire.

"So boys," Ed begins between mouthfuls, "what's the verdict, you driving up Saturday morning or camping Friday night?"

"Just the morning," Kyle answers quickly. Soon he's up and out for another bag of milk. Jason works through his potatoes.

"This race is super." Cheryll picks up the slack. "Should be just packed."

"Yeah," Jason perks up, "Radio says two thousand runners are already registered."

"Racing to an island."

"What are you hoping for?" Ed asks.

"Fifty." Jason speaks first, narrowly crowding out Kyle's "low fifties."

It's been two days since the realization run, and neither of them has broken silence. The car's a given, but in Kyle's hands. Jason didn't know until this very moment over chicken and potatoes whether they'd drive up to camp the night before or crawl out before dawn.

"Morning, good," Cheryll pronounces, "we'll do beef strips and linguine Friday night."

They leave at four to make the seven a.m. start call in Cape Jourimain. The drive north could have been pleasant, slow fog curling amidst rugged hills. As is, Kyle extends his control from steering wheel to stereo, fast-forwarding compulsively, changing tapes incessantly and occasionally doing percussion with his thumbs on the steering wheel. Jason feigns sleep or stares out at the passing stars, the crushing dawn. A blind sun rises, and traffic funnels into a steady stream of cars. Months and years worth of self-propulsion sit trapped beneath seatbelts and behind blinking tail lights. Somewhere in the distance a bridge of virgin concrete joins two provinces, catches the first sun and begins its lifelong affair with the wind.

The fitness demanded by the race rubs a healthful cheer over a check-in operation that would otherwise seem militaristic, given the scale, the rented tents and the roaring generators. Twenty-five hundred runners arrive by car to pick up their numbers, toss belongings into courier trucks and pack into shuttle buses. Jason and Kyle have each brought a magazine for the long lineups. The chilly field smells of trampled clover and gasoline. Tent flaps crumple and snap in the wind.

A fleet of jostling yellow school buses ferries runners to the start area. The shore is unassuming, an otherwise dead end that just happens to burst into concrete song. The $800-million Confederation Bridge contests the sky, bites its thumb at the wind and snubs the tide. Months and even years later, Kyle will follow the bridge's story through articles and books, impressed by the satellite positioning of the bore holes, aware of the three dead workmen smashed above or sunk below.

At nearly one-third of a marathon, BridgeRace is designed for the mid-distance crowd. The opportunity to run between provinces, however, has apparently tempted many from the short-to-no-distance crowd. The congregation looks like a market profile for Runner's Choice stores. Jason raises a thigh alongside blade-like veterans. Kyle has joined a pack of lonely fanatics running blazing warm-ups back and forth on a service trail. The design of certain sneakers rivals that of the bridge itself, and the high-tech crowd sip power syrups while programming their digital hearts. Diehards in grey trackies and flayed shoes grunt and toughen themselves as if still running after school laps for Coach Shopowitz. Returning to the throng, Kyle prefers those with a sense of humour — the chiselled Beckett look-alike in the tuxedo T-shirt, the woman in a coonskin cap. East of the bridge, two ferries plough through their swan songs.

A loudspeaker hidden behind TV vans begins to mumble. Anticipation flashes through the crowd like a neurological command travelling the length of a dinosaur. Jason and Kyle make no pretence of moving towards one another in the crowd. The day's tight schedule demands that runners still on the bridge after two hours will be picked up by support vehicles. Kyle pictures gleeful Shriners armed with pitchforks or Animal Control trucks on double duty. Two news helicopters repeatedly sweep the sky. A few fishing boats bob on the distant water, spectators perhaps, or maybe mourners.

A pistol shot tears the dawn. The collective body jerks forward. The two lanes of the bridge squeeze twenty-five hundred runners into a kilometre-long crush of limbs. Crowded beyond any organizational expectation, late buses continue to arrive for the first half hour of the race. Yellow doors open for impatient runners who lost a race to traffic.

First a hill. The concrete colossus grapples the serpent of collected runners. Around kilometre four, staring at the crowded line ahead and listening to the panting chorus behind, Kyle sees the race as the favourite clash of physicists and mythologists, an irresistible force meeting an immovable object. His brother's back hangs in front of him.

Competing Islanders, brave souls who boarded five a.m. ferries to New Brunswick to cross for the run home, have the advantage of anticipating the bridge's halfway hump. The entire sixth kilometre is a sharp rise and fall. Hearts pound like old furnaces, and all around strategic positions are lost and gained. The conversations around Jason simply stop as the incline increases. No one has the breath to question whether the hump is designed for increased strength, maximum clearance or pure malice.

Two fears spring out of Kyle's pinched sides as he struggles into the hill. One, the distance between him and Jason may be greater than assumed. Or two, Jason may actually be accelerating up the hill. Kyle tries to lengthen the reach of each leg, lever each foot. Lower on the half-kilometre hill than Jason, Kyle knows his distant brother has already endured more of this lung scour, more thigh melting.

A magnetic field keeps the brothers apart. The distance between them refuses to change as time and terrain slip by. Kyle's latest signpost reads 8 km. At kilometre nine, he discovers the ocean, the sun-drenched endlessness of it, the high nostril scrub. He is losing, but fast, clean, winged in the air. Propulsion burns beneath him while his brother's back pushes on to make a trophy of their father.

His Spaniel Skull

Affection's mingling tears were ours
Ours too the glance none saw beside;
The smile none else might understand;
The whisper'd thought of hearts allied,
The pressure of the thrilling hand.
— Byron

The air in Hanif's Toronto loft folds continuously, as if the ceiling fans are mixing a cake of delicious nothing all day long. He wakes for the third time, blinking slowly, heavily, in the late morning sun. His slim legs squirm in the large bed. Seven months ago he'd shared a one-bedroom basement apartment in Montreal. Lived off welfare. Wrote every day. Forcing off the covers, Hanif slides into a pair of warm sandals, still glad to have to walk some distance to the toilet.

He doesn't drink from the Tropicana carton but with it, strolling about the kitchen with the carton in one hand, a small glass in the other. Finishing abruptly, he drags a clean thumb and forefinger to the centre of his cool bottom lip. The walls are still too distant, the floorboards rampant. Arriving with one (borrowed) car full of clothes, books and small things, Hanif was originally crushed by space. The fifteen- and twenty-foot ceilings stole his breath. He glanced behind him constantly. Worse at night. He fled to cafés, bars. No one could write here.

Ben readjusts his earplugs and lowers his keyboard onto his lap. Bits of jaundiced stuffing fall out of the two-decade-old mucus-green lounge chair as he leans back. Ben is writing the contemporary urban romance of a subway turnstile and a commuter's palm-top computer. The turnstile is fiendishly jealous of the commuter's watch and umbrella. The palm-top is nervous about the discrepancy in their sexual experiences.

It's one a.m. The kids in the downstairs apartment settle into their thirteenth hour of loud television. The scag upstairs is well into the third quarter of her Tuesday-night drunk. Almost two hours ago a man climbed the stairs with a case of beer under each arm. Since then they've been singing three-and-a-half songs and occasionally screaming. Closing his eyes, Ben rubs a frustrated palm over his Prussian buzz cut. The dark half-inch hairs bend and give, already too long.

Running Boy started as an instant success, then improved exponentially. Hanif worked the book fairs. He read to his speckled bathroom mirror before doing the mid-size libraries. London. Waterloo. Kingston. The steady sales of the first few months surprised even his publisher. But steadiness was at least comprehensible. Now he's taken to lunches that cost more than he used to pay in monthly rent.

The only way he can bear the deluge of mail is to play with it, piling it higher and higher on top of the rickety phone table Robert left behind. The magazine interviews are no longer for queer or Asian magazines. Disney is phoning. Disney is taking messages.

In his third month of an MA at USM, Ben is still unsure about both the university and the city. The *Kama Sutra* cannot be removed from the USM library. He had to read it there, in a special room with hard chairs and tables that probably didn't conceal his erection. The attendants chewed gum and chatted about what she was like and what he was like, and then he went, and then, like, she went.

Perhaps it was twenty years ago when mail more regularly wore the stamp *Photographic materials. Do not bend!* Hanif would dip into the pile for an envelope like that. Some gratuitous home porn might even counterbalance the Gay Asian Writer mail. Dear Culture Worker. Dear Writer. Dear Fighter. Just last week Jonathan told Hanif that decades ago the government warned Kodak of impending "secret" nuclear tests so their own valuable negatives wouldn't be in transit beneath a mushroom cloud.

He looks over the envelopes as if checking the pamphlets of a small-town tourist office for good kitsch. Sewing Bea's Quilting Lessons. Tawp Dawg Water Skiing. USM English Department. Hanif winces as he remembers gleefully signing the USM reading contract four months ago. He glances at the phone without opening the envelope. A contract. What could his agent really do? He slides a finger into the envelope. One photocopied page from a book and a printed card unfold in his hands.

Son of a bitch! Son of a bitch! The scag upstairs is yelling, piercing through Ben's earplug silence as he's just inches from *les mots justes* for the sheath of germs that covers each dull arm of the subway turnstile. Muffled as these bellows are, Ben isn't sure if they're insults, compliments or some tortured form of laughing. Ben has only recently discovered that emergency wards are busiest on the night after welfare cheques are received.

First Hanif goes for the heavy ecru card.

> We are surrounded by Hyacinths & other flowers
> of the most fragrant nature, & I have some
> intention of culling a handsome Bouquet to
> compare with the exotics I hope to meet in Asia.
> One specimen I shall surely carry off, but of this
> hereafter.
> > — Byron, in an 1810 letter to his
> > friend Charles Skinner Matthews

Asia. Asia. Asia. Page 189 unfolds more easily than its prose.

> T. Luper, *The Sword and Its Sheath*

Byron begs us to recall the etymology of *allusion*. The late Latin verb *ludere*, to play, provides English with not only allusion but important neighbours such as illusion, delusion and collusion as well. *Allusion* is further empowered by the startlingly apt mid-Latin prefix *al*, meaning "to touch lightly."

Byron's sly allusion to Eumolpus is, however, more than a playful stroke. Risking both financial and social exile and criminal prosecution by invoking the sodomous "hyacinth," Byron literally plays with his life. Rewarding those aware of Eumolpus's sustained and flagrantly sodomous use of "hyacinth" to signal intercourse, Byron divides his readers with both camp and, dare I, collusion. Like the celebrated cocktail-party reference to "a friend of Dorothy's," Byron's hyacinth allusions are double entendres of the highest degree and formalize his infamous bisexuality.

Hanif flutters the two papers between a thumb and forefinger.

The phone number for Sub Rosa Flowers was easy enough to memorize. Ben glances out the window as the phone rings. Two boys in once-white T-shirts shove each other between parked cars. A ball patched with electrical tape has rolled against the curb.

"Hi, Ben Stalen —"

"Oh yes, the indigo hyacinth."

"Right, everything's okay for Friday? No cold snaps? Shippers aren't on strike?"

"Mr. Stalen, we do weddings, we do funerals, we do babies. We can do a hyacinth."

"Four-thirty then?"

"Have a nice day."

The florist hangs up feeling entirely justified that early Friday afternoon she will drive to a public greenhouse to buy a four-dollar hyacinth. She'll wrap one stem in wire and green tape. Ben Stalen will pay $17.50.

Hanif boards the plane, irritated and a-quiver. He eagerly looks into the face of each flight attendant, waiting for a sly wink, a knowing nod, a letter hidden in the lavatory. If Pilot Jim comes over the intercom to announce they're now fifteen thousand feet over a field of hyacinths, at least then Hanif will know the game's afoot.

The plane squeezes to a halt on the tarmac. Hanif half expects a chauffeur with a coded sign. *George Gordon. Running Boy. Eumolpus.* Instead, a quick-speaking woman in sensible shoes sidles up, briefcase bulging.

"Hanif Roy, welcome, welcome, Bev Durant."

Hanif doesn't hide his grimace as he follows her combination of yesterday's bad fashions and arid, bookish jokes to a nearby Subaru.

Ben can't arrive too early, but he needs a seat with total visibility. Aisle would be best, six to ten rows back. He strolls into Dougall fifteen minutes before the reading. The bottom corners of his overcoat sway a little as he threads his way through the brown upholstered chairs. Except for the first two, the front rows are nearly all locked up. Socialist Ben longs for hired thugs to clear him space. Crossing to the aisle, he tries surreptitiously to confirm that the overcoat safely covers his boutonniere. An overcoat. Who wears an overcoat to a packed auditorium? Might as well have written *Sniper* on his back in thick marker. *Nutter. Flasher.* Students with ambitiously enormous knapsacks, frayed jeans and water bottles of various sizes occasionally glance his way, thinking, he's sure, *perv*. Finally he feigns a limp and leans forward to two chatty girls at the end of an aisle.

"Excuse me, would you mind shifting over. Game leg here," Ben implores, patting a thigh. *Torn ligament*, he meant to say, *torn ligament.* Ben settles into the chair with one hand guarding a lapel. For a few minutes, he remembers to keep one leg thrust into the aisle.

Hanif is all eyes walking into the packed and breathy Dougall Auditorium. Fortunately he's used to looking without knowing what he's looking for. The only son of self-made Indian immigrants, Hanif had a puzzle, then a secret, for a childhood. He himself was originally shocked when his fantasizing mind's eye lingered over the long thighs of an imagined man. The women were always blurry, always moving out of the way. Until they weren't blurry but busy, until they were men. Hanif scans lapels and faces. Navy blazers come up empty. Smiles and grey eyes reveal nothing. He takes the reserved seat nearest the podium.

Unwilling to turn around and gawk, Hanif watches the door as a few last-minute stragglers peel off coats and rush to single seats in the rear. A few times he tries lowering his head, but his eyes dart sideways in seconds. A fashion show of vintage clothing and large shoes slowly marches by. Nothing. Fresh sideburns float past. Nothing.

Ben pats a handkerchief across his shining brow and tries not to worry that his back might be gleaming with sweat. What good is this ridiculous coat, anyway, if the boutonniere rhythmically leaps off his chest with each pounding beat of his heart? Ben raises the handkerchief again just as a hush sweeps through the room. Hanif and entourage make their nods as Ben mops his sopping brow. His damp groin stirs. He tugs the overcoat for the eleventh time and tells himself to stop being so obvious. The fire exit's the closest. Would its alarm really sound if it were opened?

Ben's body is well into overtime. Irate dwarfs hammer beads of sweat through his forehead. His heart threatens to smash right out of his chest and leap away like yesterday's red frog. Chest blown, Ben will topple, impaling himself on his own erection.

Hanif's going to blow the whistle. Look, Drs. Durant and Rao are fuming. This isn't going to be a reading but a quick witch hunt. *Before we can begin, a grave and shocking matter must be put to rest.* Hyacinth friskers will hover around every exit, and Ben's without a cyanide capsule. Dr. Durant ascends the stage.

Hanif's naked back would be like a blend of kidskin and rayon.

"Good evening, everyone, I hope you enjoy this very special evening with Hanif Roy."

Hanif stares at his shoes and silently drums his thumbs and fingers on the back of his book. There was a time when he sympathized with the difficulty of these introductions. But every glowing newspaper article and pyrotechnical window display devoted to "our" Hanif Roy makes tomorrow's work more difficult. His fifteen minutes are ticking, and it wouldn't matter if he wrote an even better book in the remaining time or described himself staring at mangos and sighing contemplatively. The passages devoted to the mango's neat, bright sticker would epitomize the developed world's labelling of the developing world, its tiny addition of value with glues and dyes. Hanif's sexuality and the spreading redness of the ripening mango wouldn't go unnoticed. He'd be equally lauded and just as quickly forgotten whether he longed for a world where things are made by hand and the post is regular or celebrated plastic and the subtle colour scheme of a Twinkie.

"And now a writer who assures us all —"

Every introduction, even one with a little heart, now feels like a boorish "Heeeeerrreeeeee's Johnny!"

"— that someone else has been there."

Ben keeps one ear on Dr. Durant and the other on the reluctant diminuendo of his heart. The dwarfs behind his forehead ease off, swap a few jokes. The fading threat of academic persecution is slowly replaced by the good old-fashioned fear of public humiliation. Did Hanif share his floricultural mystery with a tittering faculty lounge?

Hanif doesn't walk to the podium, he swims, fish-like, two sides of swishing muscle. With one elbow on the podium, he leans, perhaps a little conspiratorially, to the audience.

"Usually I start with a few jokes, you know, a funny thing happened to me on the way to the publisher's. Unfortunately, though, I've been reading the newspapers, and in Canada that can do a lot to your sense of humour."

Ben's organs are wired in series, ready for the detonator. Why is Hanif smiling? Look at that smile.

"So, quite serendipitously now, I've got a little epigraph to share. Some of you might know the "Thirsty Road" chapter, but you may not know that it was once called "A Sensible People," a title I took from a Byron epigraph I didn't relinquish until the printer's door. Since our incisive press have taken to calling me the Brown Byron, I thought I'd take this chance to give old George his nod."

Squirming Ben never anticipated an offensive defence.

"In 1810 Byron writes to a friend: 'In England the vices in fashion are whoring and drinking, in Turkey, sodomy and smoking. We prefer a girl and a bottle, they a pipe and a pathic. They are a sensible people.'"

The strength with which Hanif reads Byron fades slowly from his voice as he slides into his own *Running Boy*. To Ben, this weakness is irresistible, a beauty mark. Twice he has seen the flicker of Hanif's teeth as lips and tongue curl and stretch.

"Every stone in the road is a stomach. Ungrateful and demanding all their lives, the stomachs have fallen whole from the midst of their starving, wandering hosts. As it falls, each stomach hears the cry of its host, and shame turns it to stone. At night the stones moan for the homes they destroyed."

Ben leans forward, ostensibly to mop his brow. Leaning back, he slides out of his overcoat, boutonniere blazing and splendid. Every word wriggles into his ear.

"All roads end in sorrow. Travelled long enough, a road begins to whisper."

Hanif's eye is pricked by a small indigo clump.

"We haunt the roads that starve us."

Perhaps once a month Ben loses everything to a book, the frayed arm of his reading chair, the drone of his neighbour's TV, the urine swelling in his bladder. There are runs of ten or twenty pages where there is no Ben and there is no book but a world spinning itself on its own finger. Not often, but it happens. Ben isn't in Dougall Auditorium, he's in Hanif's mouth. He is the soft palate as it rises and falls, the reaching tongue.

"Thank you," Hanif concludes.

Ben barely hears the public questions. *Autobiographical, minority* and *marginal* breeze right past. Professorial eyes may be considering Ben anew. Cock-chugging jokes could be circulating at his expense. Like a mountain climber giddy with oxygen, Ben practically has to kick each leg with the other to keep himself moving in the book-signing line. He doesn't fumble or blush madly. He's sure, at least, of his effort.

The brown fingers which reach for Ben's book end bluntly, wildly, each nail bitten to the quick. Hanif's smile broadens at the sight of the dripping hyacinth and then cools to a thin but inviting line. His eyes flare before fading to a slow burn. Ben feels as if they are pushing against him for weak spots. The air is still cooling from these smiles as Hanif opens Ben's book to the protruding ecru card with his address and number. Is Hanif reluctant or glad to lose Ben's gaze as he bends to write a quick inscription? Ben almost draws back at the vulnerability of Hanif's hair and skull as he bows over the book's title page. Ben doesn't read the brief inscription until he's safely out of the building. *Soon, Ben, soon.*

Showering, Ben rescrubs his crotch and suffers the anxieties of murder. In his youth he did an Agatha Christie binge. The Duchess of Murder herself assures Ben that the oftentimes disturbing behaviour displayed by a murderer upon arrest does not indicate madness but the simple torture of secrecy and failed planning. Unravelling months of work and private rehearsal in seconds could unhinge anyone. Ben watches the last of the soap rinse past his ankles. Every second brings Hanif closer. His every step, across parking lots and down cracked sidewalks, is toward this damp pink body.

Ben crosses the living room in a towel. Steam and the cedary scent of his soap dissipate through the air of his small apartment, air which grows increasingly heavy with the weight of an anticipated knock. If he'd been trying to seduce a white girl, he would have burned sandalwood incense before she arrived.

Hanif's back follows him into the room repeatedly as Ben dresses. Pulling a tight black T-shirt over his head, Ben sees both his hands throwing the lock over and over again. The lock will click like thunder, warning every neighbour of impending filth. Women have been over on flimsy excuses. He's made and received telephone invitations for midnight strolls and late-night teas. When a woman's on her way, Ben thinks of what might happen. Checking the stack of bedside books one more time, he wonders what will happen to him. The inescapability of high-school wrestling isn't entirely forgotten. Bodies still slither through pain, will and fatigue until one finds victory.

He paces. He checks the clock. He wishes he smoked. The

quickest, most tenacious traps always risk catching the trapper too. Weeks of deliberation draw an increasingly famous set of skills, desires and expectations to Ben's door. He could bolt. Hide out in a pub. Crash at a friend's.

The main entrance to the building creaks open. Steps pad across the carpet and assume the stairs. Ben's is one of two apartments on the second floor. The steps end with a brief knock.

Despite himself, Ben opens the door to colour. Skin, skin, it's what he sees. Flax seeds. Deserts of cocoa. Beauty flies to Hanif's face and clings there for its life. His rumpled white shirt is pulled out of his trousers.

"I'm glad you found your way."

"I think it's your way I found," Hanif replies, holding up the Byron card like an invitation.

They step in and Ben throws the lock.

What? What? Drop to my knees, hike his shirt and munch stomach? Grab a clump of hair and go vampiric on his neck?

"Wine? Scotch? Beer?"

"Okay, I'll take the whisky, thanks."

"All right, find us some music." Looking back from the kitchen, Ben watches Hanif bend over a CD rack, revelling in the speed with which ass becomes back, becomes thighs, becomes hips.

"Ice, Hanif?"

"A little, please."

Ben returns to some slow Beck. The room's half-dozen candles catch in the Scotch and the ridges of each glass. Ben does meet his eye while presenting the drink.

"Not much, I know," Ben pronounces, sweeping a hand toward his panelled walls and gnarled carpets.

"I'm used to it." Hanif wags a finger at the bookshelves. "You're studying literature?"

"Trying to."

"So what about a list of favourites?"

"Well, Faulkner, Christ, he just *had* suffering."

"Sure had something."

"You don't like —"

"Never really given him the time."

"Conrad? I just reread *Heart of Darkness*. Really is amazing, despite itself."

"Meaning?"

"Well, Chinua Achebe talks about Conrad fetishizing blackness. A man rising on black legs, extending black arms, stretching a black neck. What, he's going to rise on black legs and extend red arms? Crane a yellow neck?"

"Actually the old sailor kind of works for me. His pink fingers dangling from pink wrists, pink ears suspended over a pink neck."

Ben suffocates until Hanif pulls back and stares at the panelling. Startled, Ben realizes they're still standing. "Please," he says, gesturing at two waxy chairs with cheap printed cloth desperately stretched over them. Ben and Hanif sink into opposite sides of their chairs while settling the inside leg over an arm. Their calves brush. Music and a few sips of whisky drift by before Ben jabs a thumb at the ceiling.

"I'm amazed we're not beset by screaming. Normally quite a cage match upstairs."

"The noise travels?"

"On frequent flyer points."

"Oh."

Ben's leg is manacled in hot iron. Each inch that touches Hanif's is bound and paralyzed by a hot, squirming feeling Ben prays isn't obvious. This pleasant torture aside, Ben sees that their postures actually send hands, shoulders and mouths off in opposite directions.

Looking at Ben, Hanif quietly ventures, "I think men get scalps."

"Scalps?"

"Men stopped wearing hats before women. Military boys. Criminal kingpins with shaved heads. I think the scalp is pretty male."

"Lots of girls go for the buzz now."

"But only today. For you a scalp's all male. And yours is a dream."

Silence radiates from the compliment, increasing in density as it ripples through the room. Panic rises quickly in Ben's lungs, like water in the tiniest of caves. Two bright pops fade from his lungs as he slides from the chair to his knees, one leg tucking under him, then the other. Leaning forward, he lowers his spaniel skull into Hanif's hands.

His ear first, the tip brushed, perhaps accidentally, perhaps not. Two, three, four different fingertips drag over the ends of Ben's short hair before they reach his crown. Each fingertip traces absently over his skull as if it were a window covered in steam. Circling, circling, the fingers finally spread apart to allow the palm in for a good rut. Another hand swoops in, sweep, sweeping back to the crunch bones of his neck. The mudslide at the back of his skull turns his face up into the candlelight, his lips higher and higher. Ben kisses back two or three times before realizing the tickling on his top lip is the brush of fine whiskers.

Ben reaches for Hanif's calf, dipping fingers through the edge of the muscle and worming a thumb just off the bone. Without looking, Ben can feel the direct line running between his mouth and Hanif's belt buckle. Even men's pants feel tougher.

The deeper they kiss the farther forward Hanif leans, rolling back tailbone and chair. Ben pulls his hand over a knee and begins an Alexandrian drive up Hanif's thigh. He squeezes skin into cloth.

Hanif sinks from his chair and slides down Ben. His erection draws across the tops of all thighs as the inside of Hanif's knees look for the outsides of Ben's. Ribs rise and fall. Ben smiles as Hanif reaches for the top buttons of his shirt. A V widens over the chestnut hairs of Ben's chest as each slipped button bares more skin. His hands dig and prowl up Hanif's sides, burrowing in a damp underarm.

Ben is on his back, Hanif a hungry mouth over him. Nipples are sealed then swatted with a glacial tongue. His solar plexus does somersaults. Abdominal muscles sway.

Hanif topples over co-operatively with a buck from Ben's hips. Buttons are all done for. Ben's straight for the goods, hauling shirt up with a fist and snarling his way across the enormous Portobello mushroom of Hanif's stomach. Reaching fingers dig into Hanif's mouth, pinching at teeth and tugging on cheek. Thumb and knuckle roll a top lip. Straddling him, Ben hauls the shirt over Hanif's head. His chest is a twitching seal.

Propped on one shoulder, Hanif pats the carpet, inviting Ben to lie down. Crossing to the door, Hanif slips the boutonniere from Ben's jacket and returns beside him. Starting at the ditch of his neck, Hanif sweeps the hyacinth back and forth across Ben's chest and follows it with a thorough mouth, as if Ben's chest were a street and Hanif the efficient machine that cleans it. Fingers jerk at Ben's belt, button and fly. The pants and shorts come off like years. Sucking, Hanif travels from hip to hip like a dutiful ferry. A furrier's fingers play and stroke Ben's scrotum. Lips enter a forest of hair. A surveyor's tongue traces the base of his sex. Pleasure climbs up him. The sweet tip dissolves.

Ben pulls away from the exquisite head for another reversal.

He gathers Hanif's pants like a desperate sail. He's just received a grand performance and reaches for his first thigh. Ben works up from the knee, wild with so much hair in his mouth. Gently sweeping aside the tackle he sets his tongue into the ropy joint of pelvis and thigh. Drawing his lips up the side of Hanif, Ben feels momentarily like a parasitic fish living on the side of a whale, content to one day swallow his home. At the top Ben takes the stiff shaft in his fingers like the legendary Chinese flute. Weeks of planning pull together into a few square inches of skin. The salty, musty taste comes back quickly on the first sweep of tongue. His lips manage the tip, and Ben warms up, sending last minute prompts to his soft palate and epiglottis. Taking Hanif, Ben has the distinct impression of diving — pressure builds, air dwindles, darkness and fear loom ahead. One mutinous tooth could end Hanif's coos. The landmark ridge passes by.

A fleshy tree trunk has suddenly been shoved down Ben's throat. Drops of saliva fall from the corners of his mouth, splashing to the forest floor below. He reworks the old ground in an attempt to relax the back of his throat, trying to push away panic with each half-inch. Flying back to the top for some distracting speed work, Ben readies himself for another plunge. Again it's too much — the orchestration of lips, tongue and the rear meat of his throat elude him. How he envies the jawless, goat-swallowing python. He can't keep resurfacing like this. Instruction is a distinct, shameful possibility. Will a man give him the tap? How do they get it all in? Think big picture. This time he doesn't fixate on his throat, praying it will suddenly flower and take the width. Ben drops from the back of his skull, imagining an X-ray as he guides Hanif into him, sinking to the hilt. High-platform diver, Ben's nose brushes a clump of hair that smells of his own saliva. A few more short-rope ascents and Hanif bucks in the small rodeo of orgasm. It goes down like raw eggs and cough syrup.

Ben rolls aside on the hinge of his hips, stretching out on the carpet, stroking Hanif's thigh. Hanif's lips soon find Ben again and chase the need through his body. Ben comes like a slow accident, a bucket of rainwater tipping into the wet grass.

They lie knotted on the floor. Candles have burnt down around them. A distant street lamp catches pieces of Hanif, pieces of Ben, in its slow yellow light.

*

Grey Hound

Andy and his dad Stan sit together on the crowded bus, racing slowly. They were racing on their way to the Kingston station. They'll race when they get off in Toronto. All of these races in bone.

Andy is thirteen years old, and soon — four to six months — he'll be taller than his dad.

"You just wait, Stanner, I'll give you progress reports on your bald spot."

"Evil, evil boy."

"Or *spots*, I should say."

"You remember what a will is, don't you?"

When Andy sees his mom — Christmas, their March Getaway — his height is always the first thing she mentions. This has been going on since the divorce, and he's amazed that, if anything, she sounds even more surprised as the years go by. He doesn't tell her how quickly Stan is shrinking.

"So how is your father?" she still asks early in each visit. Same, he mumbles. By the time she's worked around to, "You're not there forever, you know?" her long, slender hands have already found papers to tidy up, grapes to wash, a present to hand over.

Stan still drives in town. The office. Strip malls. Always the dry cleaner's. For years Andy thought that's the only way men's pants got cleaned. Small errands, yes. A drive into Toronto, impossible.

Once a year they devote a whole day to thirty minutes with Dr. Khan, one of the specialists. Andy couldn't tell you whether Khan is Neuro or Rehab, OT or PT. In fact he doesn't even know the name of Stan's disease. If it were something internal, a hidden workers' strike in the pancreas, a length of intestine blown like rails in war, a name might help carry him inside. But here, arms bent and ruinous, one leg torquing out, the other locked in an ice of bone, what's in a name?

Travelling for more than an hour, Andy feels entirely coated in bus, slick, infectious bus. He cannot avoid multiple conversations about what someone reckons is a good idea for starting up a business and what They say about this, and They now say about that. Although the ride there always feels longer than the trip home, nothing is as biblically interminable as the wait in Dr. Khan's excessively bright sitting room. The hands on the beige clock don't move any faster than the orange squares and green cones of the office's huge, ugly painting. Each year, dark, ambitious weeds grow back on the asphalt-covered rooftops.

"Okay," Stan declares, "let's go." He drops his copy of *Time* to the gummy bus floor, and Andy knows they're in for another mad rush.

First you've got to get him up. Andy steps over Stan's swaying, scrawny knees and into the aisle. Surging with the pitch and roll of the bus, Andy steadies his legs and reaches down for Stan's hands, finally looking into his face. A drawstring of alarm has tightened around each eye.

It will be another year or two before Andy understands his father's binary bladder. Yes, he knows Stan's sense of touch is diminishing radically. He grew to expect the sight of infected, dime-sized lesions on Stan's fingers long before he actually saw his father's clawed hand brush a red-hot stove element. Dad, your hand. Oh, damn. Maintaining balance, Andrew now knows, is a largely visual operation. Still, what Stan's weakening arms can or cannot do is the main battle. Pulling up pants on a cold morning. Managing a large sandwich. Inside, inside is a foreign worry, each organ continents away. A crisis pee, well, that's just local colour compared to food, clothes and standing upright. So many shop windows are smashed nightly that neither of them notices the backroom legislation seizing all assets. Really Stan's only feeling extremes, inside or out. A half-full bladder isn't even noticed. Three-quarters is a nag he can't place.

Stan's arms seem to fade a millimetre or two each time Andy hauls him up. Mid-route between sitting and standing upright, Stan's hands and arms begin to pull away from his chest. Andy has to arch his spine, bend his knees, step back if he can, to take up the slack. Sometimes Stan's arms lose so much ground Andy feels as if he is pulling straight up, hauling a fallen Hollywood man back up over a high-rise balcony. Stan's too-vertical arms look as if he hopes to fly out of his seat.

Upright and fully evolved again, Stan exhales victoriously before proceeding to battle-test his legs and knees, high-stepping from one foot to the other. The brown scrubland adjacent to the 401 rushes past on either side. The bus drones, drones.

Andy has pulled Stan up in the only direction he can, toward the driver. The washroom, of course, is in the rear. The long march back cannot begin until they manage a one-eighty. Two children begin to stare. A pale woman wearing a headscarf averts her eyes. A man in a plaid bush jacket clenches his jaw. Andy wonders whether they look like an indivisible unit, a them, or whether they actually look like two people standing face to face, a pair of backs in the middle of the bus?

Unnecessarily, Stan looks into Andy's eyes and nods. Okay, round two. Twisting and tugging Stan while propping him upright, plucking one leg, guiding the other, Andy waves his tiny ass in all their neighbour's faces. Excuse me. Sorry. Just be a minute here. Successfully reversed, all hands locked, Andy checks once behind his feet and prepares to roll.

"Damn."

Andy follows Stan's gaze to see the washroom's *Occupied* sign light up red. A tiny girl stands on her seat in yellow rubber boots and looks unapologetically from the sealed door to Stan and Andy, then back again. She wears a green dinosaur T-shirt. Eventually a mother pulls her back down.

"Just keep stretching." Andy keeps his own knees slightly bent for the roll. While Stan's gaze never leaves the *Occupied* sign, Andy's alternates between it and the driver's wide mirror. Visor-like sunglasses. Walrus cheeks. Ginger moustache.

The intercom coughs awake. "I'm sorry, sir, there can be no riding in the aisles."

Stan would have ignored him fifteen minutes ago. His feet shift too often. C'mon, c'mon, he mutters.

"Sir, absolutely *no* riding in the aisles."

Between glances, Andy pictures the bus pulling over to the roadside, the walrus driver hauling flab from the seat for a mid-aisle showdown. He stops looking forward. Drone, drone goes the brown land.

Finally the washroom door opens. Stan jerks Andy's arms like a horse's reins, not noticing Andy is already stepping back.

Part owl, part minesweeper, Andy cranes his neck from side to side as he pre-checks each step and gauges the stability of Stan's feet with each passing glance. Step left. Step right.

Stan sees the large middle-aged woman in a cat sweatshirt step out of the washroom before Andy does. The three of them cannot, will not, share the meagre aisle. Stan keeps driving, shifting their legs, one-two, one-two. Andy casts a net of hope to each side, scouring the averted heads for an empty seat. Stan's grunts change gear and pitch. Full to the left. Passengers will have to double up, stand crotch in a stranger's face. Stan's every movement is propelled by a high buzzing note at the back of his throat. The dinosaur girl's hair is as blond as a June dream. Andy doesn't see the free seat on the right until the cat woman lowers into it. His sigh is internal, silent.

Flattening himself between Stan and the unfortunate passenger tucked into the seat beside the washroom, Andy holds back the spring-loaded door with first a hand and then the raised toes of one foot as he guides Stan in ahead of him. Stepping as far as he can, Andy steadies his uneasy father with both hands and doesn't watch as he lets the spring-loaded door shut against his own outstretched leg. Wrapping Stan's fingers around a knurled safety rail, Andy presses himself into a corner before reaching back for the tiny bolt of the token lock.

"C'mon. C'mon."

Reaching under Stan's arms, Andy tries to ferry him across the few remaining inches to the stainless steel hole of a toilet. A sudden turn threatens Stan's besieged balance and shifts his whimpering into overdrive. "In the sink. In the sink." The rectangular mirror shows him nodding his head between crotch and metal bowl.

"That's where people wash their hands."

"The zipper. Hurry. Pull it out. Pull it out."

Andy has to turn his head and burrow one cheek into Stan's left shoulder blade in order to reach. Glancing around, Andy sees them half-reflected in the steel walls, toilet and seat. Only Stan can see the actual mirror, precise reproductions of buttons, belt, zipper, meat, and his eyes are closed, beatific. Andy looks from the many versions of their humped, greasy reflection to the blue floor's coin-sized circles of raised rubber. Traction is improved. Spills are contained. Collected near the neglected toilet are dark hairs and aging, viscous stains. Andy tries not to listen to the urine slide over the smooth steel of the sink. The sharp bones and thin muscles of Stan's back relax steadily against Andy's cramped cheek.

"Sorry, Andrew. I won't forget this."

"Makes two of us. Finished?"

"Yeah, all done."

Andy packs his father away.

"Better hit the water."

"I'm not stupid."

The tap opens to nothing. Again and again Andy screws and unscrews the tap. Nothing. Should the walls cast accurate reflections, Andy's furious eyes would meet Stan's for just one second before the bus takes a severe bump. Instead, two pink orbs trade vague stares before the big hit, and Andy shoots his hands out reflexively. One hand grabs Stan's chest and the other the nearest good grip. His left still holds Stan after the tremor fades from the bus. He slowly withdraws his dripping right from the pissy edge of the sink.

"Oh, Andrew —"

"Shut the fuck up."

Twice Andy scrapes his nose over Stan's back while searching for paper towel, Handi-Wipes, anything. Voices can be heard from the other side of the door. Andy wipes the counter, sink and hands with thin scraps of quickly dissolving toilet paper, then flushes the whole mess in a blue swirl.

Him Not Me

"No, no. Out Montreal. Back 15."

Nathan and Andrew both look up but neither speaks, so Marc presses on.

"Think about 15. We climb then descend a hill. We pass the base and RMC, they're sentries. We cross the droning skeletal causeway. Water on either side."

"No, that's just what I'm saying," Nathan shoots back. "That's our exit. The causeway's a bottleneck, right? Going out Montreal, that's just car trouble. We go out 15 and we've got to get past RMC and the base, then they're sentries."

"Fifteen allows a detour up the fort if we want it," Andrew chimes in. "Depending when we drop, we could even do sunset at the fort."

"Around tourists and faux nineteenth-century soldiers? No thanks."

"You were a faux nineteenth-century soldier!" Andrew and Nathan throw pillows, casual fists.

Drop, walk and stroll. They've decided their little acid reunion should be a walkabout. Montreal Street and Highway 15 are the upper and lower jaws of the Rideau River as it enters Lake Ontario and the St. Lawrence. Montreal comes right into the main street and yet ten k out are farms and junkyards; 15 meanders through orchards and forests between Kingston and Ottawa, striking one straight run from the self-absorbed 401 until its end at CFB Kingston. Both following the widening Rideau, Montreal and 15 make the distance between them at that cross street — the one with the lock — much shorter than that in town. "We fly open jaw."

"Out and back. No bubble kids. No fishbowl restaurants. No bristling townies."

"The lock? Do you really think climbing in the dark while peaking is such a good idea? All right, I guess, yeah."

"Climb the rock. Run the fort. Dead City over the 401."

"In."

"In."

"That'll work, Andrew?"

"Yeah. It's all right."

Andrew is on a leash of time. He always declines a pint after a three-hour night class. Some Friday nights, he readies his father for bed as early as seven p.m. Before he leaves, late as usual, Andrew installs Stan at the kitchen table, spreads the newspaper before him, turns on the hall night light. With the table, Stan can manage the paper.

Just the two of them, they need support, emergency contacts, communication. That these things are being finalized so Andrew can secretly drop acid when Marc and Nathan return at Thanksgiving is beside the point. Safety first. With a system, there's no reason Andrew can't be absolutely unavailable, unhelpful for eight or ten hours.

The cartoon parodies are not wrong, LSD'll toss you up on

beaches you didn't know existed. Walking out Montreal Street in the dark, however, makes this a little harder to realize. Perhaps under the squiggly light of restaurant fluorescents, Andrew, Nathan and Marc would have enough breathing skin, flowing fabric and peripheral squirts of colour to ease back and let the drug take control. Walking out of the city with only the distant twinkle of a few isolated houses ahead of them or the fading smear of the city behind forces all of their hallucinations into the swelling cones of passing headlights. Flashed with this quick, infrequent light, they have no time to dwell, no time to wonder at what they're seeing. Just as vibrations, limbs or colours start to form inside a light, they're gone. Forced to march single file on the roadside, the three friends are not awash in bubble gum hallucinations but doused with doubt, and doubt doesn't need any more ground. Doubt's already got cold fingers between your ribs as you wait between the last digit of her phone number and the sound of her voice. Your house key will someday taunt you with doubt. Milk bags weigh doubt white. And yet the collegiate drugs — hash, weed, shrooms, acid — overflow with doubt. Buy it. Swallow it. Don't be surprised when you meet it in the passing cone of a headlight. Andrew doesn't say a thing about the bent, impaled men shoved deeper and deeper into the night with each passing car.

Turning off Montreal — eight, ten k out — they sink into the even greater darkness of that cross street no one can name, the bowl-shaped one with hills at either end and a lock in the middle. Walking down that first hill, Andrew starts wondering about his legs and periodically swatting his ears. There, the right, yeah, yeah, there the down, no, the down-up, yeah, that's it. A tiny limp flickers in one leg. In an instant he switches from wondering if he feels it at all to being unable *not* to feel it. A small twitch every time the foot's off the ground. Perhaps it's nothing, a perpetual spring turd ready for the flick. Or is it coming from the ankle? The knee? It may be spreading.

With traffic largely abandoned, jokes spring to their mouths. Colour seeps back into their eyes. By the time they hit the wide lawns surrounding the lock, most of their feet purr.

Imagine an enormous bathtub made by a giant stonemason. Make it even bigger and you've got a marine lock. Tip over a freight elevator for good measure. Canadians have run across the land replacing waterfalls with stone elevators: A vessel approaches and passes the open Gate 1 to nose up against shut Gate 2. Gate 1 closes creakily to create Chamber A (bordered at either end by shut Gates 1 and 2). Gate 2 opens just a little to allow the water in Chamber A to flow by manageably and slowly fill Chamber B. When Chambers A and B finally share the same water level, Gate 2 is opened to allow the vessel passage through Chamber B to shut Gate 3. And so on and so on.

Lying along its stone edge, staring into its black waters, Marc, Nathan and Andrew are lost in Chamber A.

"It's not nature. It's a fucking shopping mall."

"'Tis the sea, b'y. Nature's stormy bride."

"The right angle meets cement. Nothing more. Nothing less."

Most locks are also parks. Picnic tables. Polite shrubs. Obedient lawns. The kids might like to ride the boat elevator the first or second time, but soon enough it's better to hop the rail, chase each other across the lawn and slide down a couple of banisters to wait at the bottom alongside the enormous black chains. Although they're usually tight, you can wiggle a few individual links with your toes.

Marc, Nathan and Andrew lie over the last edge of grass, stomachs flat across a prefab sidewalk, faces dangling just beyond a thick lip of cold iron. A strong erratic wind whips about the lawn behind them.

"Hello, Death." Marc stares down into the still dark water of the lock. "Who's a good death? Huh? Who's a good death?" Reaching farther and farther, he extends his palm down to the bobbing sealskin of water.

"Did you feel that?" Nathan asks, glancing back at the grass.

"No," Andrew lies, his heart jackhammering into the concrete and iron beneath it.

Nathan peers into the empty darkness above the lawn. Marc pets the water. Andrew tries to soothe his twitching leg.

"There. Again." Nathan persists.

"Death, death, death, death." Marc with the petting.

In his mounting terror, Andrew doesn't have time to decide if it's better or worse that Nathan also feels this hunger, this stalking behind them. "Nothing," Andrew claims. Through the dark. Over the bending grass. One claw and a paw, a peg and one fin.

And then Marc is over, screaming into the dark water.

The screams drown first. A death of sound: the scream ending in a sudden splash, the shocking silence. In Nathan or Andrew's peripheral vision, that was just an otter sliding into the water. But now silence says everything. The shock has already faded across the lawns, dissipating along with the ripples of black water.

Nathan and Andrew spring to their feet. Life ring? Gaffer? Long branch? Terror comes up from the lock in rectangular sheets to smash whole in their faces. So Andrew leaps, reaching one hand back to tug Nathan down with him. The cold dark water is a one-two punch that gives you just enough time to anticipate the second blow but not enough to avoid it. Cold slices your ankles with its left hand before smashing you over the head with a stone right. A truly three-hundred-and-sixty-degree environment, a complete sleeve, an utter volume of cold. The entire head is bandaged in biting strips, and for two, three, four falling seconds Andrew has forgotten about Nathan. And Marc.

Your eyes can do nothing but sting. Your body's sense of its own top, that internal gyroscope, is your only hope. The throbbing orb of LSD wears a fresh coat of panic. Andrew leapt, so his lungs are as inflated as they can be. He comes across this air like money in the pocket of an old coat, noticing it just as his descent slows from the force of his leap to gravity alone.

Even the water's resistance is a function of cold. The ever-cutting blade sharpens with every inch. No matter how far down he has come, a void of colder black remains at his feet. Pulling an ancient summer camp lesson through three brands of fear, Andrew sweeps both arms upwards as if to clap them godlike above his head. Plunged down still farther he sends ballerina legs out in opposite directions, probing for big soft lumps. Rusty manacles of every kind pop into his icicle mind. He claps down farther, half certain he'll wedge himself into a rusting oven. *En pointe*, he searches fore and aft one last time before fear bounces off the ropes and comes back swinging. The slow, methodical legs of the search shake off their concern to thrash back and forth. Somehow the flurry of legs doesn't seem to push the skullcap of cold any closer to the surface. Up, up, and still he must go farther. The cornered rabbit of his heart is ready to detonate in a skinned ball when a different blade of cold slices at his face. He is in the air, rushing with air.

"What the hell are you doing?"

Andrew must draw Nathan's fury along with his first sweet breath. Their slick beaver heads bob in the dark water as they tread and float.

"Marc? Where's Marc?"

"Back down looking for you. Aaaaaggghhhh. Tripping without one little murder just not enough for you?"

"How long has he been down?"

"Long enough for me to lose another toe to the cold. What the hell was that about?"

"Let's get out first."

"Well, thanks, Cap, now I know what to do. How? How do we get out? No lines. No ladders."

"This is Canada. Of course there's a ladder."

Marc bursts up, gasping. "Nothin — there's the fuck."

"Me? You're the trend-setter here."

"Hey," Nathan chimes in, "the only one here who isn't a complete asshole is me. *Can we please get the fuck out?*"

Funny, but lake means house. Here at the bottom of a valley, at the intersection of lake, lock and river, liquid begets solid. Small cottages and three-storey homes ring the small lake.

Being early May, the warm, promising days are still followed by a backward-glancing chill each night. Shivering now, Marc, Nathan and Andrew stop and start in various directions, crumbling into a double-barrelled panic of cold and mind-warping drug.

"We've got to move. I can feel the cold spreading through the ground and up my feet."

"The mother ship has already implanted us. Nothing can stop the virus now."

"You're both queens. We make a stand." Marc leans over to speak to the ground in front of his feet. "Out here, the cold worm needs hours to reach our hearts."

"Right. Let's move." Andrew.

"Wrong. Let's fire." Marc.

The scrub brush surrounding the lock supplies enough fallen, dead branches to keep a fire going for a week. The park lawns are studded with free-standing iron cooking grills. They won't run out of wood. They won't burn the forest down. They don't have any matches.

5

Booze is crime's common denominator. The violent start walloping. The lecherous drop their pants. Theft comes to the minds of those it shouldn't to replace stealth with shades of oblivion, invincibility or apathy. Whether the country is hot or cold, the violence marital or martial, alcohol is de-evolving. We become loud takers. If Marc, Nathan and Andrew were drunk, they would struggle toward the secluded lakefront homes as thick-skulled hunters and gathers. But this is Lucy's show. Their senses are anything but numbed. The geometry of a mailbox could snare any one of them. Texture is captivating. The million skin of tree bark. Leaves, tapestries. Molars of gravel chew at their feet. Need to cock an ear? Throw it up a tree. Yo-yo your eyes down a lane. They are not brash and obvious, they are invaded.

"Smokers are the last Boy Scouts." Nathan is the mastermind behind Operation Pinto. "Car lighter. Flickable Bic. Matches. It's about contingency."

Relatively speaking, pharmacologically speaking, the fact that all three of them are still advancing on the same parked car is utterly amazing. They have all swapped paperback tales of magical lands in which travellers stumble upon hypnogourds. The runty gourds have pips which seem, why, yes, like perfect little eyeholes. To stare into a hypnogourd is to be lost in an alternate, eternally stalling dimension. Straight down Jacob's ladder until someone or something breaks the line of sight between pip and peeper. Marc, Nathan and Andrew are all lost in their own gourds and still they fan a blue Nissan.

Every car is dead. Dead skins stuffed and stretched. One, two, three cars locked tight as vaults. All with marmalade eyes. Without the drug, it would be obvious why the cars farthest from the lake and closest to the road are most likely to be locked.

"Move out, soldier."

One, two, three, Andrew's up again. *I fell. He got sandbagged.*

You leapt. You're the striker. Crunching over the gravel of the driveway, he tries fake tai chi. Carry the Tiger to the Blue Nissan. The red grid of the rear defroster is a pressure-loaded net.

Heart in his mouth, ghosts after him wet or dry, Andrew clears the rear taillight. One quick step past the fender and wham, the phrase hits him again. Heart in his mouth. The oyster of his own soft palate. A sprawling mussel inside each cheek. One foot in front of the other, wind rushing leg and back, Andrew realizes he is eating his own heart. Slit shark, he can taste the coppery salt of the blood in his own face. Gag and vomit reflexes kicking in, he is unprepared when the passenger door opens in his hand. A ferret caught in the thin yellow rectangle of the interior light, a wolverine, a spinning circle of snarling teeth. One claw and a paw, a peg and one fin.

In the interrogative Nissan glow he spots a pack of DuMauriers and the only way out. Stepping into the car he draws the door shut after him — not tightly but enough to kill the light. Lost now to Marc and Nathan, pupils still scurrying from the dome light, he fumbles in the dark. His fingertips trace upholstery packed tight with dirt, finding pennies, pen caps and receipts but no matches. Popping in the car lighter should have been his first task. Dipping into a side pouch overflowing with maps, he can already see himself getting caught, one unlit cigarette dangling from thin, bloody lips. Pop. He steals fire from the red coil.

Approaching Marc and Nathan silently on wet shoes, Andrew hands over the coveted cigarettes, declares, "I'm not eating meat anymore," and walks on, lock-bound.

Six cigarettes lit one from another. Three to keep an ember, three to ward off the chill here in Rome. "Makes perfect sense. You're cold, bring the fire inside," Nathan mumbles, puffing away contentedly. Andrew draws on, spilling the rank nicotine over his tongue and down into the tall, pink sacks of his lungs as his father's body screams across the night. One claw and a paw, a peg and one fin. No, he cannot be left behind.

Hiding there just beyond the circle of firelight. Andrew steps closer to the raised fire of the iron hibachi, unable to suppress a full body chill, a foot-to-head jerk that comes from knowing it got his father from the inside out, bumped down the roulette wheel of spinal nerves to take parts of each arm, leg and hand, to corrode the sense of touch when it could have just easily grabbed sight or hearing. Bobbing its way from cell to cell. From cell to cell.

Slightly different versions of the following stories have
been published in various periodicals: "Profanity Issues,
S" in *Prism*; "Sitting Up" (as "Tomorrow's Soldier")
in *Exile*; "Grey Hound" in *Zygote*; "Enormous Sky White"
(as "Apples That Don't Want to Get Eaten") in *broken
pencil*; "Non-Violent, Not OK" (as "Kwump, Kwump,
Kwump") in *The New Quarterly*; "Kermit Is Smut"
in *Dandelion*; "A Sharp Tooth in the Fur" in *The Danforth
Review*; "The Body Machine" in *The Windsor Review*;
and "I Iim Not Me" (as "A Peg and One Fin") in
The Fiddlehead. "Sitting Up," "Kermit Is Smut,"
and "To Take a Man on a Hill" appeared
in *Coming Attractions '98* (Oberon).
"A Peg and One Fin" won the 2000
David H. Walker Prize for Fiction.